Andrew Meikle was one of the youngest of the 12 original members of the highly successful Uncle Toby's Ironman series, established in 1990. For eight years, Andrew consistently finished in the top ten, one of only three athletes to do so. During these years, Andrew spent hours of training with, competing against, and observing, Australia's elite athletes. He began to question why the most naturally gifted athlete or the hardest trainer didn't always win and what made the winners different from the rest. He also began to examine why winning didn't always make people happy.

In pursuit of the answers to these questions, Andrew embarked on a global journey to interview world-famous athletes and outstanding achievers in the business and medical worlds about their beliefs, and uncover the strategies behind their success.

As a result of his research, Andrew established his own philosophies. Through his company, 'The Meikle Files', and various other projects, he shares his winning philosophies with those who want to discover how to happily achieve rather than just achieve to be happy.

Andrew's new philosophies and technology have had outstanding results with many of Australia's largest companies, including Westpac, Lend Lease, Woolworths and Lexus. Much of Andrew's time is also spent working with elite athletes and the Australian Institute of Sport.

Win Now, Win Later is his first book.

WIN
NOW
WIN
LATER

WIN NOW WIN LATER

The 20 Principles of Happily Achieving

Andrew Meikle

HarperCollins*Publishers*

HarperCollins*Publishers*

First published in Australia in 1999
by HarperCollins*Publishers* Pty Limited
ACN 009 913 517
A member of the HarperCollins*Publishers* (Australia) Pty Limited Group
http://www.harpercollins.com.au

HarperCollins*Publishers*
25 Ryde Road, Pymble, Sydney NSW 2073, Australia
31 View Road, Glenfield, Auckland 10, New Zealand
77–85 Fulham Palace Road, London W6 8JB, United Kingdom
Hazelton Lanes, 55 Avenue Road, Suite 2900, Toronto, Ontario, M5R 3L2
and 1995 Markham Road, Scarborough, Ontario M1B 5M8, Canada
10 East 53rd Street, New York NY 10022, USA

The National Library of Australia Cataloguing-in-Publication data:

Meikle, Andrew, 1970— .
    Win now, win later: the 20 principles of happily achieving.
    ISBN 0 7322 6642 4.
    I. Success - Psychological aspects. 2. Self actualization
    (Psychology). I. Title.
158.1

Printed in Australia by Griffin Press Pty Ltd, Adelaide,
on 79 gsm Bulky Paperback

9 8 7 6 5 4 3 2 1
02 01 00 99

DEDICATION

To Mum, Dad, J.P. and Peppi.
Thank you for your belief. It makes the road
so much smoother.

ACKNOWLEDGMENTS

I would like to thank Sam Meikle for his creativity and talent in taking the paint, and creating the picture. I am grateful for the dedication and talent he displayed in editing my draft manuscript and shaping it into the book I wanted it to be.

To Monique Schwitter, for her unfailing faith and strength.

Also a big thank you to Geoffrey Schucraft and the I.Q. team for their support and action, and Alison Urquhart at HarperCollins*Publishers* for her under-standing and flexibility.

And to my parents — all three of them — Suzie, John and Les, my gratitude to you is endless.

TO THE READER

Since the beginning of time, people have been searching for the 'truth' and what is 'right'. I do not believe there is one 'truth' that is true for everyone; and I know that what is 'right' for some may not be right for others.

This is why I am not promising my book will deliver you the 'truth', but rather *information that works*. I have seen it work. *Win Now, Win Later* is the result of a decade of research during which I have asked the questions: What is it that enables a person to manage that fine balance between being happy, and achieving at their best? How do the people who can accomplish this actually do it? What is it that makes a Happy Achiever?

The principles in this book are the essence of what I believe makes the difference between someone who wins gold medals and someone who happily wins gold medals. I hope as you read you find some ideas that are 'true' or 'right' for you.

— Andrew Meikle

CONTENTS

INTRODUCTION

He had a million dollars in his cash-card account alone! This was a man I'd been looking forward to meeting for weeks. He'd made so much money, and so ridiculously quickly. The other thirty or so million was enough to fulfil any dream or cater to any whim that took his fancy. I was fascinated to know what made him tick. The questions consumed me: What set him apart from everyone else? What did *he* do that was so different? What were his strategies? What did he focus on, the money or the achievement? All the late nights and early starts — what drove him to go that extra yard? As usual, my challenge was to make the best possible use of my time with him, and that meant asking him as many questions as he could stand in that time.

The search ... that's what makes me tick. It's an obsession. As a professional athlete, I'd naturally assumed that the best way to improve my results was to learn from the best. It had all started with world champion athletes. How did they do it? But it wasn't long before I knew it was more than that. What about surgeons, surely they could give me the answers? If *they* cracked under pressure, someone died. Or business achievers. With so many young entrepreneurs trying to make it, what made the achievers different? I wanted to know how to achieve.

The answers I'd gathered over the years had taken my breath away. I'd unearthed something new from every conversation. A new concept. A fresh idea. Fantastic strategies. I was sure that if someone else, anybody else, applied these strategies, they'd work just as effectively as they had for their originator. I wondered how my millionaire's personal strategies would compare to the others I'd discovered in my earlier interviews.

The similarities are a constant source of amazement to me. If the athletes are following similar strategies and principles to the surgeons, the business high-fliers and the artists, then the possibilities are limitless. *If all of us who strive to create something special could just follow these same principles, we would experience so much less frustration, so much more momentum.*

I remember the feelings that were back-flipping in my stomach as I approached the mansion. A cocktail of excitement, expectation and, if I'm honest, a little fear. Would he open up? Was I getting in his way? What if I came across as stupid? I breathed through it. A pinch of fear keeps you sharp. The house was huge. It loomed like a church. As I glanced around the yard, it struck me that the place hadn't been touched in a long while. Another question popped into my head: How had he been able to make the time to see me? I kicked through a pile of junk mail, scaled the four creaky steps and pressed the doorbell. There was a distant ring. 'Be there in a minute,' his voice echoed back at me. He was there.

While I waited, I happened to look to the left and about a hundred metres from where I was standing was the garage. A pile of fallen leaves lay on the open tilt-a-door, undisturbed. It hadn't been closed in a long time. Inside sat a wind-blown, grimy, red Ferrari, its sleek exterior looking the worse for wear. I remember thinking that I'd never seen a dirty Ferrari. They're usually the pride and joy of their owners, shiny as the day they rolled out of the showroom. My fear was gone, replaced by rising curiosity.

A man in his early thirties with a long mop of unruly hair that grew straight up in every direction greeted me as the door swung open slowly. 'Come in.' His voice was soft and cautious. He looked tired. Lost. 'I haven't cleaned in a while. Don't mind the mess.' We made our way down a hallway cluttered with magazines and long-forgotten sporting equipment. 'We'll talk in the living room,' he mumbled as we passed through the kitchen. I was dying to look in the fridge, betting that I'd find ancient Chinese take-away and milk that had gone sour. This early in the meeting, though, a peak into his fridge would've been a little too forward. But my curiosity was growing.

The living room was sparse and cold. A pinball machine stood in the corner, buried under a mountain of yellowing newspapers and more ignored sporting goods. A couch sat in the middle of the room behind a coffee table, again barely visible under piles of old magazines and papers. A state-of-the-art racing bike my triathlete friends would've killed for leaned against the couch. 'You do some cycling?' I asked, to get the ball rolling. 'Used to. Haven't been out for a while.' This seemed to sum up everything I'd seen so far.

I was conscious of the time, so I launched into my questions. I wanted to learn how to achieve, I said. How had he done it? He'd started with nothing, he explained. He had realised, even as a child, that if you have no money, you have no freedom. He was only moderately enthusiastic as he explained where he had come from, where he had been and where he was now. But he seemed to enjoy the chance to explain to me, if not to himself, how it had all happened. However, as I listened to him I got a strong sense that I wasn't getting the whole story. I felt that there was more he wanted to tell me, but that he wasn't quite ready. I'd have to be patient.

I knew that I'd take away many valuable things from our conversation, so as it drew to a close I was content to let it wind up. I'd expected to find a happy, thirty-three-year-old, Ferrari-driving millionaire. Instead, he seemed somehow dark and disturbed. I was sure he wanted to talk further, but our time was almost up.

'I can't thank you enough,' I said, as I began to pack up my briefcase. I was in awe of how much he'd achieved in so little time, and even more amazed by how unfulfilled he seemed. As I stood to leave, he surprised me by asking: 'Are you in love?'

The question stopped me in my tracks. His tone was more assured than at any time during the two hours we'd already spent together. 'Yes, her name is Monique. You?' I sat back down, hoping he would finally really open up. 'I was. Not any more.' The same tone I'd heard when I asked about his bike crept back into his voice. 'We broke up six months ago.'

And so began maybe the most valuable hour of my life to date. We started to talk, and this time he spoke from the heart with passion and honesty. 'At two o'clock this morning, I gave up trying to sleep. I realised if I was going to follow through with this, I should do it now. I started to think of ways I could kill myself.' I was stunned … speechless. A happy coincidence, because now he seemed to need to talk. I know now that the conversation that followed was about timing. If the Mormons had knocked on his door, they may well have had the exact same sixty minutes.

He told me more about the last few years, the achievement years. About the search for love, for happiness, for fulfilment. He hadn't found it. He confided that he'd been sure that achieving the monumental goals he'd set for himself would bring him what he wanted most: the feelings of happiness, success, confidence and, most of all, freedom. He felt as if everything had slipped through his fingers, and now he was self-destructing. He wanted out. No use cleaning the Ferrari, or raking the yard, or staying fit. No use going after any more goals, they only lead to heartbreak. He was at the top of the heap, but felt empty, at rock-bottom.

I've spent time with genuinely suicidal people and he wasn't going to kill himself — that night, or in the future. He just needed to give voice to his feelings, to the desperation. I stayed until I was confident that he was safe, then thanked him and left.

I was in a state of shock. Our conversation had left me reeling. All my life I'd focused on achieving, on how to turn what is intangible into something I could reach out and hold on to.

My brain was scrambled. I started to question everything — everything I'd believed in and felt was important. I saw so much of myself in him — the drive, the intensity. I wanted to achieve for the same reasons of freedom, happiness, success, power and confidence. I realised, for the first time, that achievement alone wasn't going to give me the feelings I craved most in my life.

It took a few days, but when the dust had settled and some clarity had returned, I let my mind drift back through the memories of the interviews I had done with high achievers over the last few years. This time I looked for something I hadn't been sensitive to during the actual conversations: *How many of those people were actually happy?* I was stunned ... I couldn't escape it.

We see them on TV, and we read about them in magazines. We eagerly await their next triumph. But we form unrealistic perceptions of most high achievers. We see happy, smiling faces. Unconquerable icons. Generally, they're in the public eye after another brilliant win or triumphant achievement. But what happens the other 99.9 per cent of the time? Images of the interviews flooded through my mind, and this time, I decided to look for that rare breed, the *Happy Achiever*. My question now became: How can I create and achieve what I want, *and be happy doing it*?

New realms of possibility and understanding opened. I began to understand why so many people achieve so aggressively and with such focused intensity, why someone would 'sell their mother to go to the orphans' picnic' in business, and why destroying the environment might seem inconsequential if all the feelings you desire in life were riding on your success in a property development. I understood the athlete taking drugs that will ultimately destroy his health, in the hope of winning. I could see the remorse of so many successful people when they realised that the extra time spent at the office hadn't been worth missing their children's development. They realised too late that achievement alone hadn't given them the feelings they longed for.

For me, life was a life-and-death game — the thought of failure so painful that I tried to block it out. It never helped. Late at night I'd focus on failure, and it frightened me into a cold sweat. The pre-race fear and anxiety was almost unbearable. I seemed to race tight and tense, hardly ever loose and relaxed. After a good race, I felt over the moon; after a bad race, I sank into the depths of despair. I'd be down for days until I had a chance to redeem myself.

The pressure I put on myself to achieve great results was overwhelming. During my races I'd get opportunities to break away and win, and never take them. What if it didn't work? What if I failed? Safer to hang back. I'd feel a lack of confidence, self-esteem and personal power. So much was riding on a good result — irrational, but true. I wasn't conscious of it at the time, but it was now so clear. Now I understood why. I could see so many things I just wasn't seeing before my meeting with my tormented millionaire. I finally understood I'd been asking the wrong questions.

My first reaction to this new world of under-standing was total excitement. I had to share my new discoveries with friends. Their first reaction? 'So, you're anti-achievement now.' 'No way,' I replied. 'I'm the exact opposite.' We need to strive to achieve. Life is 'juicy' when we are passionate and intense, when we feel focused and have to rely on emotions like courage and faith. Achievement means we have to stretch, we have to solve problems, to conquer fear. *Achievement is a tool for personal growth.*

We need big, fat, juicy goals to inspire us to make a difference, to make the short-term pain associated with any worthwhile goal worth enduring. By having a reason to push through the pain, we grow as human beings — we develop and become more resourceful. And when we develop, we give ourselves the best possible chance of being happy. But achievement is a *process*, not an *arrival destination*. A goal is a tool that helps us to experience juicy emotions throughout the journey to accomplishment, not something to help us feel those emotions on arrival.

What if we could *happily achieve*, rather than achieve in order to be happy? What if we could *successfully achieve*, rather than achieve in order to be successful? What if we could *achieve with freedom*, rather than achieve in order to be free? What if we could all achieve in a *more balanced way*?

I wanted to find a way to win/win/win. *Win now* by spending my time fulfilling my emotions. *Win along the way* by achieving my goals so much faster. And *win on arrival* because I am fulfilled, not empty like my millionaire friend.

Many hours spent talking with highly successful people and thinking about their strategies for success and happiness have brought me to this point. I've sought out the Happy Achievers and used all my resources to find out how they do it. Specifically, I wanted to know if there is a set of principles that creates the Happy Achiever. There is.

What you are about to read is the fruit of my research, the twenty principles I have found that sets the Happy Achiever aside from the Unhappy Achiever. As you read, let these principles make a difference, let them be a call to action. Some times the smallest action can have the most amazing impact.

I'm sure we can all achieve more if we can experience the emotions that are most important to us *now*, rather than setting ourselves up to experience them later. I've found the traps of the *unhappy achiever set-up*.

My motivation and drive was, and is, to live my life to the ABSOLUTE MAXIMUM. Every day in my work I run across the unhappy achiever, so every day my passion to help people see what I now see, grows. I want to share with you what I've found, and I want to thank you for giving yourself this time, for taking a leap of faith and having the confidence in me to deliver. I won't let you down. My goal is simple:

To show you a way to achieve at your absolute best, and to have a ball doing it.

My heart is with you.

LOOK FOR THE LIGHTER SIDE

If a person's reputation precedes them, then his reputation rolled out the red carpet for him long before he arrived anywhere. He was a Happy Achiever of the first order, and the current world champion. We had only ever met briefly before, and this time I wanted to get to know him. I wanted the chance to learn from him.

We use the term 'world champion' without really understanding what it means. More than any other human being on the planet, he was the *absolute best* — the master of his chosen sport. The really interesting thing was that his reputation spoke of a man whose entire focus in life, even more than winning, was *having fun*. Of course, often this resulted in him appearing in the winner's circle, grinning as he sprayed the crowd with champagne.

I'd seen him race poorly on TV, but he always finished, no matter how embarrassing his final place.

Other champions might pull out, not wanting their reputation to be damaged by a bad result. But not him. He'd cross the finish line with a smile, congratulating the competitors who'd beaten him, his smile and the warmth in his handshake completely genuine.

Although our chosen sports were different, this particular week I'd be racing him three times in a unique format combining our two events. Ten of us had been flown to an island to compete head to head. I'd decided, a few weeks before, to retire as a professional athlete. I would fulfil my contracted commitments, then move on to attack my new passion which required my undivided attention. So, for me, it was a great opportunity to observe some fantastic athletes in a pressured environment. It was important to race, but it was more important to learn.

'Not another damn watch!' A packaged gift box flew over our heads and into the bushes. He'd arrived. The 'damn watch' was actually a two-and-a-half thousand dollar gift to each of us from the sponsors. We all quickly looked over to find him laughing uproariously. 'Hi, guys!' He then disappeared into the bushes to recover his gift. We all enjoyed the joke, which broke the tension. He'd taken the pressure off for everyone. Straightaway, I knew I needed to find out what made him tick. I watched, listened and learned.

During the race, he got so cold he was taken away wrapped in a space blanket with mild hypothermia. He finished last. How would he handle it?

I saw him later at dinner, where he refused to view the race in negative terms. Sure, he'd gotten cold, but tomorrow was another day. It wasn't that serious. The night went on, and he joined in the fun and laughs. People gravitated to him. I think he reminded them of what it's like to be a kid, what it's like not to worry. His emotional state hadn't changed with his poor result. I was amazed.

I'd met another athlete with a similar make-up, also a world champion, a few years before, and the expressions on their faces were identical. It made me think back over my races in years gone by. The hour before the start, the time spent in the competition tent, was the hardest. All the competitors had to assemble in the tent before the race started. It kept the onlookers away and provided some privacy in which to gather our thoughts in the few minutes remaining.

There would be thirty-five or so chairs arranged in a horse-shoe formation around the interior of the tent. I'd look around and see pale, blank faces, drained of blood. Several of the guys would have towels over their heads to keep their focus from shifting to the other competitors. I'd see athletes wearing headphones to block out any intruding noise or voices, their eyes wide open, their focus turned inward. I'd see uncertainty in those faces, self-doubt and self-questioning.

One day I realised what I was actually seeing, and it hit me like a truck. I was seeing fear. So many of us were terrified of failing. At that point, failure was as serious as death. Life was way too serious.

In contrast, when I looked at the champion, the man who'd won more races than anyone else in the history of the sport, his smiling face told a different story. He'd chat with a few friends around the fringes of the tent, completely calm, a peaceful power radiating from every pore. He seemed under control in an uncontrollable environment. He'd start the race loose and relaxed, without every muscle fighting the others for the right to win.

A very simple attitude was having a massive impact on both world champions. The effect on their results, and on their quality of life, was far-reaching, and from that first insight on the island I've made the principle behind it a major focus in studying Happy Achievers.

Before we get to the principle, I'd like to look at the fear of failure. If someone came to me and said, 'I want to know how to stress myself out and give myself the best chance of failing', I'd suggest to them that they fear failure. This emotional pattern turns us around and does exactly the opposite of what we're trying to achieve in this book. It teaches our brain that no matter how good things are now, we should worry about the future. I've done a lot of interviews with very affluent people who are captives of their wealth because they are scared of losing it.

Fear of failure teaches us that action is fraught with danger. The world is full of 'potential people' —

people who sit on great ideas, wonderful scripts, amazing inventions and awesome achievements, because they fear the possibility of failure. They fail to act on their inspiration, because fear kicks in right from the word 'go'. Sometimes it won't even be a conscious decision; they just won't get around to it.

~

IT'S HARD TO BE HAPPY WHEN YOU HAVE UNFULFILLED POTENTIAL.

~

Fear of failure teaches us that taking a risk isn't an option — there is too great a chance that things won't work out. One of the essential elements in Happily Achieving is a willingness to face risk and to condition ourselves to enjoy the uncertainty. Risk is present in every juicy activity, right through our public, personal and business lives.

~

IF YOU'RE NOT RISKING ANYTHING, YOU'RE NOT ON THE RIGHT TRACK.

~

Doing what scares us, helps us to grow as human beings and as achievers. Fear of failure, on the other hand, doesn't allow us to explore our potential. Worst of all, it teaches us to tear ourselves apart inside. It creates the awkward and ridiculous situation where we actually have to fight ourselves if we're going to achieve. A part of us knows we have massive potential, but there is another part that is unwilling to discover it. With that much inner conflict holding us back, it's almost impossible to be consistently happy.

~

HAPPILY ACHIEVING IS ABOUT CONQUERING FEAR.

~

Fear of failure is created when our brain, based on our past experiences, associates failure with massive pain. Our brain's number one priority is to avoid pain, so when someone fears that failure will lead to pain, it follows that their brain will try to avoid failure at any cost. On face value, that doesn't sound too bad, does it? It sounds like their brain will map a path through the minefield of possible failures and they'll come out the other side achieving all they set out to do. The problem is that the strategy the brain uses is a blanket strategy: Avoid! Don't go there! Go back! Fear! Don't try anything! The brain can be very inventive in avoiding pain.

A person with this mental set-up will sometimes achieve, but rarely do they achieve happily. They're in a constant state of terror at the possibility that failure is lurking just around the next corner. Some people never start things, because their brain reads starting as taking a step closer to failure. Some do manage to start, then don't follow through and finish things, because their motivation drains away mid-task when they realise that by finishing, failure becomes a possibility. And other people create a massive stress pattern, unconsciously believing that stress will keep them sharp and signal to them when failure is approaching. The trouble here is that the stress can end up running riot and feeding itself, even when things are going fantastically well.

I recently did some coaching for a guy who was stressed about trying to get the job he wanted. When he got the job, he was stressed about being able to keep it. When he got a pay rise, he was stressed about investing his money wisely. I asked him, 'If you survived a plane crash, would you be stressed about losing your wallet?'

It's easy to find yourself in this cycle in a world where the opportunities for security are on the decline and competition is increasing. This guy's internal set-up was the exact opposite of the world champions'. Regardless of his achievements, he would never find fulfilment unless he decided to change.

We must learn not to take everything so seriously. Many people react to this by saying, 'You can't just act as if everything's OK, when it's not.' That's a good point, but I'm not suggesting for a second that we should walk around with our head in the clouds, ignoring situations that need our time and attention, in the belief that there is no point in getting wound up about things. That way, we just end up being completely ineffective. Rather, it's about having a focused, controlled, peaceful power at your command, like my world champion friend does, so that whatever is going on, you find you can smile under pressure.

Not too long ago, a man stood up during one of my presentations and asked: 'How can I *not* be serious about all the serious problems in the world?' Even though I was half-joking, my answer summed up the problem with this way of thinking. 'You know, I agree with you. There are so many sad, frustrated, unfulfilled people out there, you should feel that way too. That'll really help you to help them.'

~

HOWEVER SEEMINGLY IMPORTANT THE STAKES, LIFE IS JUST A GAME.

~

The best way to compete well in this game of life is to have fun by always looking for the *lighter side*. When we were kids, we all saw clearly what happened when anyone playing a game took it too seriously — they'd end up stamping their feet, throwing a tantrum and bursting into tears. As we grow older, these behaviours don't change that much; they just become more sophisticated, and we attach different labels to them — 'being stressed', 'being highly strung' or 'having a bad temper'.

The lighter side principle is about being driven, passionate, ambitious, focused and courageous, but at the same time taking a light-hearted approach to life. It's about taking massive action in order to fulfil our dreams, because, while failure might hurt, it isn't like death. It won't stop us from going for it. We must risk failure if we are to go where we want to go. Every significant achievement in the history of the world has been made at the risk of failure.

When it comes down to it, failure isn't all that serious! The lighter side principle reminds us that we will wake up tomorrow, and that every day has unlimited potential.

The lighter side principle says that knowing failure is a possibility just makes the experience juicier. If we knew that we would always succeed, then achieving would be boring. There wouldn't be any fun, because we would never enjoy the feeling of being surprised. The lighter side eliminates the fear of failure, because the brain's association of failure with pain dissolves. When we realise that failure is just another player in the game, a player that will only occasionally rear its ugly head, that's when we really learn how to play.

The serious approach says, 'I've failed before, and I'll probably fail again', stopping any action dead in its tracks. No action, no momentum. The lighter side approach says, 'That really hurt, but my potential is unchanged. What's next?'

The lighter side is a commitment to enjoy the process of achieving, making fun a priority. So many people have forgotten what life is about. Surely, with all the great things there are to do, see and experience in a lifetime, we must have been put here to enjoy as many of them as we can, and to have as much fun as is humanly possible.

One of the simplest, and yet most effective and important, lessons I've learned through my interviews is to do what works, what gets good results, and not what fulfils only your emotional needs. It's like the person who fills his or her day with unimportant activities that contribute nothing to the bigger picture. They want to give the impression of being busy, because they believe that busy people are important people. The same applies to getting too serious in life.

Sometimes it's tempting to take things too seriously, because it fulfils certain emotional needs, but it doesn't work as an achievement strategy — not now, for our emotional state as a whole, and not later in terms of the results we passionately want to achieve.

It doesn't help our chances of achieving to look at life in a serious way. Happy Achievers live and work on the lighter side. I wonder if you would have a better time, if you'd be happier, and if your journey would be smoother and so much more fun, if you could approach life from the lighter side? Would your personal relationships improve? How would your friends react to you? Would they loosen up and start having more fun around you?

The only way to know, is to try it and observe the results. Try applying the lighter side principle to your life for one week. If you catch yourself taking things too seriously, remind yourself to lighten up. This is a simple process I call 'C&C', or 'commitment and conditioning'.

~

START EVERY CHANGE WITH A COMMITMENT, THEN FOLLOW THROUGH WITH SOME CONDITIONING.

~

A week will be long enough to show you how this principle will work for you. I'm absolutely sure it will, and it's important that you feel it for yourself. Before you go any further, do a C&C. Make this book work for you. My goal is for you to be Happily Achieving by the time you finish this book, but it's up to you. Make the commitment and condition this principle now. If you're unsure where to start, try asking yourself these questions:

~ **What would next week hold if I decided to start it with a light-hearted approach?**

~ **What new action would I take if failing at it wasn't that serious?**

~ **What would happen in my life if it was just as important for me to have fun, as it was to achieve?**

GET CONSCIOUS!

His face told the whole story. It was the sort of face that warned an explosion may be only moments away. Danger! Go back! His face hinted at many secrets, and I sensed that he could turn from laughter to slaughter in a heartbeat. If this man threatened you, you stayed threatened. So I was curious about why he'd requested that I spend an hour in his company.

'I'll tell you the story,' he said, taking control and barely giving me time to take a seat in his office. There'd be no small talk that day. 'I've got some problems with anger.' He went on to explain the events that led him to ask me for help. Story after story followed about fights he'd had with his staff — not just yelling matches, but actual physical fights.

I spared a thought for his employees. It's hard enough working every day with a moody boss, let alone one who would give you a right cross if you lost a sale. 'How's your staff turnover?' I asked. His look sent a shiver down my spine, and I made a mental note not to try any more jokes until we'd fixed his anger.

He went on to describe the event that had finally pushed him to pick up the phone and call me. He'd been driving his car, a throbbing V8 anger machine, to work the previous morning and another driver in a yellow street machine had made the mistake of cutting him off. This unforgivable act required vengeance. He pursued his quarry for several kilometres, until they stopped at a set of traffic lights. He described what happened next with an unsettling lack of emotion. 'I saw him stopped at the lights and something snapped. I just planted my foot on the accelerator and rammed into the back of his car. It was like I couldn't control it.' He softened. 'Neither of us was injured. We were lucky.'

'Well, it does seem like you have an anger pattern,' I said, forgetting the no joke policy. He fudged a little chuckle and I breathed a sigh of relief.

We were able to rewire his anger pattern fairly quickly and, noticing that I had a few minutes to spare, I asked him the same question I ask a lot of the people I meet. 'What do you really want in your life?' He replied without the slightest hesitation. 'I want to be Prime Minister of this great country.'

An uncomfortable silence closed in on us as I searched for an answer. I was stunned, but not because he'd set himself such an incredible goal. I encourage massive goals because of all the juicy emotions that we experience in going after them.

I was stunned because so many of the emotions he'd demonstrated *didn't support that goal!*

Then it dawned on me: he wasn't choosing his behaviours; he was just running an old program. Whenever a situation came up, subconsciously he would just flick a switch and the system would take over.

One of the keys I've discovered to the Happy Achiever is that their behaviours support the achievement of their goals. Pretty straightforward, right? Not necessarily, because achieving this congruence in behaviour can be a real challenge in itself.

To understand this, we have to understand how behaviours are built. I believe that the majority of our behaviours are learned. Sure, there are certain survival-based responses we're born with. A classic example is the 'fight or flight' syndrome. In situations involving stress, our heart rate naturally increases to enable us either to combat the danger or to flee from it. That's a given. What I'm saying is that the vast percentage of the things we do and the ways in which we react are learned, and learned from a very young age.

We learn from our parents, our friends and our teachers, by watching and experiencing, through trial and error. As we grow, we develop a 'file' on how to react in most circumstances, and so every one of our behaviours is designed to achieve a certain outcome. Everything we do, we do for a reason, even if that reason isn't evident; and, basically, each behaviour either keeps us away from pain or leads us to pleasure.

By the time we reach our early teens, most of our core beliefs and behaviours have been built. We've learned to cry, or not to cry, in certain situations, to get angry or to stay calm in others. We've discovered whether we like to fit in, or prefer to be different. We've decided whether promises are to be kept or broken. And we'll have developed behaviours to get or to avoid love.

By this stage, the human being is well on the way to being built. We are all individuals, because each of us has had our own unique developmental experiences. We are the sum of all the experiences we've had thus far in our lives, *unless we challenge them*.

~

WE ARE THE SUM OF OUR PAST, UNLESS WE DECIDE NOT TO BE.

~

The flaw in the brain's system for designing behaviours is that it doesn't allow for evolving goals. The behaviours we learned as a five-year-old to get an ice cream won't necessarily win us the business deal. In other words, the approach we picked up years ago may not support our current goals. My car-wrecking client was using behaviours that had worked for him, or that he'd seen work for others, at some stage in his life. To put it mildly, these behaviours didn't work in his present situation, and they certainly wouldn't suit the office of Prime Minister, should he achieve it in the future.

His subconscious conditioning was running his behaviour. It was as if he was allowing an old, outdated program to run his new computer, instead of installing a new program more suited to the tasks he now wanted to achieve. When I first noticed the 'old program' strategy, I wanted to study it for a while. I saw so many people tearing themselves apart inside because their behaviours were running them, instead of them running their behaviours. So, I started with the first place I'd seen it — in myself.

I remember as a kid I loved nothing more than to watch TV for hour after hour. It gave me massive pleasure. Then, as an athlete, I'd watch TV during my recovery, killing time until the next training session. At the time, watching TV was a pretty suitable behaviour for pleasure, and then for recovery.

Then, about two years ago, I took the time to notice just how much TV I was watching. When I added up all the hours I spent in front of the box, late at night and on the weekends, it came to about twenty hours a week. I suddenly realised the cost. What if I added that time to the time I was already spending in researching and developing other concepts?

I pulled out the goals I'd written down earlier in the year, and I couldn't ignore the fact that this behaviour wasn't suited to the life I wanted to create. My goals are incredibly ambitious, to say the least.

Yet, I was running an old program and I hadn't even noticed it. I was just doing it because I'd always done it. I needed to 'rewire' it. That didn't mean giving TV away; it just meant bringing the behaviour back into line with my goals — and not watching *so much* TV.

I found a whole swag of behaviours that used to work for me but didn't fit any more: the way I treated people, the way I reacted to bad news, the way I worried about things, the way I could never say 'no'. So many changes needed to be made. I was getting increasingly frustrated with myself for not achieving my goals as fast as I wanted to, and this frustration was making my sense of happiness and achievement even more elusive. I realised that the speed with which we achieve our goals comes down to *the behaviours we use every day*.

I made this concept the focus of the next few interviews I did with Happy Achievers, and the strategy they used to ensure that they were moving at absolute maximum speed towards their goals I called *getting conscious*.

The achievers who had mastered this were in a constant state of questioning. How can I best react to this situation? Is what I'm doing the best way to get it done? I didn't like how I treated that person this morning — how could I have done it better? The essence of their strategy was to identify the behaviours they used every day, to become conscious of their habitual reactions. The bottom line is that we must monitor our thoughts and behaviours constantly. We have to become actively conscious, and place a gap between what happens and what we do about what happens.

If we react without conscious thought, we are put at the mercy of our conditioned behaviours. We have to stop running the old programs and learn to make conscious choices.

Some people are fortunate enough to have their past produce exactly the behaviours they need to Happily Achieve. They do it so well, they don't necessarily need to get conscious. But most of us need to replace our old behaviours with new ones designed to help us achieve our goals happily and quickly. We need to monitor our actions and reactions, and adapt them to suit what we want *now*.

~

AS WHAT WE WANT CHANGES, SO MUST OUR BEHAVIOURS.

~

It might help to think of ourselves as being like a pot of soup, simmering away on the stove. What needs to be added to make it taste really great? What ingredients would spoil the taste? Are there any character traits I should throw in? What would happen if I added some relentless drive to my soup? What if I dropped in a handful of courage, a pinch of understanding, a dash of flexibility or a cupful of passion? What if I removed the seriousness and strained off the fear? Would the soup then be delicious as well as nourishing?

I want to make absolutely clear the difference between the principle of getting conscious, and the way in which most people operate. The achiever who is conscious first designs the *outcome*, and then designs the *behaviour* that will *achieve* that outcome. We must remain constantly aware of who we are and what we want to do, and add new behaviours or remove old ones as required.

The frustrated achiever sets a goal, but doesn't consciously design the behaviour to match. He is forever fighting himself and getting down on himself, because he's not doing what it takes to achieve what he wants. Often, this is blamed on a lack of motivation. It's *not* a motivational problem. The frustrated achiever is definitely motivated, but he's not acting consciously. He's busy doing the wrong things, the unimportant things, and yet he can't understand how someone can work as hard as he does and still not achieve what he has set out to achieve.

I estimate that the chances of being a Happy Achiever who doesn't *also act consciously* are about eight million to one. The answer is that we must get conscious. We must monitor and adjust our thought patterns and behaviours, as appropriate, every minute of the day, so that we're not at the mercy of our past. If we are to Happily Achieve, we must be willing to constantly redesign ourselves.

Not long ago, I sat down with my journal and wrote in it the question: 'Am I the person who will be able to achieve what I want to achieve?' I had been scared to ask myself this, and the answer that I came up with shocked me: No, I wasn't. However, the process of asking opened the door for me to start getting somewhere. I asked myself more questions, and the answers gave the soup a whole new flavour. *Sometimes it's not until you ask the really disturbing questions that the answers show themselves.*

Try these questions. They're a great way to discover if you need to get conscious of who you are and what you're doing.

~ **Is there a gap between the person I am and the person I need to be to achieve my goals?**

~ **What do I need to add to become the achiever I know I can be?**

~ **What do I need to take away?**

PRINCIPLE THREE

MAKE YOUR DESIRE
UNCONDITIONAL

Seven years ago he'd been two million dollars in debt, his business had been in ruins, and he'd been looking down the barrel of starting from scratch. Sitting in his Sydney apartment, he worked out that over the following year he'd have to make half a million dollars before he could keep a cent. He borrowed the money from a friend to buy a computer, and then he sat down and designed a brochure for his new business. Seven years later, he had ten million dollars in the bank and was free of debt.

We'd met after one of my seminars and decided on the spur of the moment to go to dinner. As we talked over our meal, I realised that this was an incredibly methodical man. Some achievers have no idea how they produce results; they just act on instinct, not allowing their mind to over-complicate things. This man really impressed me, because he knew *exactly* what he was doing, how he was doing it, and why he was doing it. He seemed to have a well-planned strategy for just about everything.

A classic application of this in his life was the fact that he'd recently married. He had set out a few years earlier to design the perfect approach to finding the right partner. He established the criteria that a woman would have to meet for him to consider her as a possible wife, and they were tough. Her parents still had to be together; she had to have a great relationship with her father; and she should be attractive and have a terrific personality.

'It all sounds a little clinical to me,' I responded. 'What about love? What about that feeling that you can't stand to spend a minute apart from her?' But he'd done his homework and gave carefully considered reasons for the criteria. Not wanting just to dismiss his strategy, I put aside my own feelings and simply looked at the results his strategy had produced.

Apparently, he'd met his wife out of the blue and, luckily for him, she fit all the criteria he'd laid out. Some of his friends had joined us for dinner, and they convinced me that he was telling the truth when he said that she loved him as much as he loved her. They seemed to be the perfect couple.

His strategy for finding the right woman had been very conscious, and so it was easy to see how he produced results in other areas of his life. Most of our meal was spent exploring how he had managed to achieve such a massive turnaround in his life.

'Do you know what people in your business tend to ignore?' he asked me towards the end of the night. Not being a shy man, he looked directly into my eyes and said, 'At the base of everything is desire. Nobody ever talks about desire.'

I got a strong sense that he was building to something big. 'How is desire at the base of what you do?' I asked.

'This may sound a little weird, but I take a very spiritual approach to my life. I believe that the universe holds everything we want.' As he spoke, his hands clenched as if he was holding a rope, part of a tug of war.

'When you desire something with your whole heart, when you want it more than anything else, and that desire is pure and strong,' he let go of the 'rope' dramatically, 'the universe has to let go and let you have it. This has been at the base of everything I've done.'

Spirituality aside, he had chosen a powerful way of illustrating what happens when we really want something, when we truly decide that there is something we have to create in our lives. Desire is a hugely neglected component of human performance.

~

NOTHING IS ACHIEVED WITHOUT FIRST EMBRACING THE DESIRE TO MAKE IT HAPPEN.

~

The mistake which many people make is that they run out of fuel before they achieve their dreams, because they don't take the time to build their desire. Creating a compelling and lasting desire is fundamental in realising sustainable peak performances.

~

ACTIONS DRIVE OUR DREAMS. DESIRE IS THE FUEL THAT DRIVES OUR ACTIONS.

~

The obvious question, then, is: Why do so many people lose the desire for what they once wanted more than anything in the world? I believe the answer is rooted in belief, or, more precisely, a lack of belief. The minute we no longer believe that our dreams are possible, the desire starts to wane. Think about it for a second. If you believed, without a doubt, that you could achieve what you most wanted, do you think that your desire to take action and chase your dream would increase?

~

WE LOSE DESIRE WHEN WE LOSE BELIEF.

~

The interesting thing is that desire doesn't necessarily guarantee happiness. In fact, it can create intense unhappiness. Desire only guarantees drive. We've all felt the downside of desire —

impatience and frustration, the disappointment that comes with falling short, the fear of not achieving what we desired in the first place. Many of the destructive emotions that we encounter on a day-to-day basis are tied up with not having what we desire — so much so, that people often decide that the downside of desire isn't worth the risk. Rather than keeping the dream alive and clear in their mind, they lower their standards or let the dream die.

I've found that the basic difference between Happy Achievers and those who focus on the downside of desire — the disappointment that comes with not achieving their desires — is that Happy Achievers *build a relationship with failure.*

~

HAPPY ACHIEVERS BUILD A RELATIONSHIP WITH UNFULFILLED DESIRE.

~

Imagine that you're in the most amazing relationship. Imagine that you love that person so much that you ache when you're apart, and being together makes you feel whole; that no matter where you are, you're home if your lover is with you. Emotionally, this is probably the riskiest situation that we can find ourselves in — our desire to be with that person comes from a place so powerful that it defies rational thought. However, whether that person chooses to spend their future with us is totally beyond our control.

Many people avoid opening their heart to this situation by settling for something that won't hurt as much if it fails. The downside of desire wins. Others will actually pursue the situation, and then spend their time wrapped up in emotions like jealousy and fear because they're consumed by the possibility of failure. The downside of desire wins again.

In this situation, Happy Achievers build a relationship with the failure of the relationship. They imagine it, feel it, explore all its emotional possibilities, and then decide that they can handle whatever pain might come with it. They accept that at the end of what could be a very painful process, they would have the pleasure of finding that special someone who would love them enough to want to share their future.

In building a relationship with failure, Happy Achievers take the unknown out of the downside of desire and confront the fear that goes with it. They don't buy into the scarcity mentality that says, 'There is only one person I could love this way.' They know that having their desires go unfulfilled isn't a life-or-death situation; whatever happens, their desire will carry them through, because *their desire is unconditional.*

~

UNCONDITIONAL DESIRE ISN'T ATTACHED TO AN OUTCOME.

~

The same principle can be applied in the business sector. For example, let's say that you really want your proposal to be accepted. With one signature, your turnover will double. The problem you face is that you will have to go through six months of checks and balances before you'll have a definite result. You're in for a wait. The question then becomes, is this going to be a happy six months or a stressful six months? Your desire is intense; however, the downside of that desire is the frustration of not knowing and the fear that it might not work out.

Happy Achievers build a relationship with the failure of the deal. They know that there might be disappointment, but they also know that they have the resources to handle it. They come from a place that says, 'If there's one deal out there, there'll be lots more.' A relationship with the downside allows desire to flourish, free of the negative side-effects that come with an attachment to a particular outcome.

Now, I know this is easier said than done. It's not something you can hear on Monday and have wired in by Friday. It takes conditioning and practice. I also know that it's not sexy when I give you a principle that takes more than three seconds to apply. I, like you, want to know how to do something as fast as possible, but developing as a human being is a life-long project — a piece of art that may not be finished when we finally leave this planet.

The state of unconditional desire is something we are constantly working towards, not something

we instantly achieve. It wouldn't be human to
believe that we could have the deal of the century
riding in the balance and not care how it turned
out. But wouldn't it be great if we could have all the
juicy emotions that desire brings with it, while
diminishing the effects of the downside emotions?

Feeling a lack of desire isn't our natural state; it
signals that something needs to change. If we are to
be happy, we have to have the *desire* to be happy. If
we are to live full lives, we have to have the desire to
improve as human beings. If we are to Happily
Achieve, we have to have a relationship with the
downside that reinforces our unconditional desire.

When you're thinking about what it is that you
most want, ask yourself:

~ **What do I desire the most?**

~ **What is the downside?**

~ **Am I too attached to the outcome?**

~ **Do I believe that what I desire is really
   possible?**

~ **Is my desire unconditional?**

ALIGN YOURSELF WITH YOUR GOAL

Have you ever noticed that some of the biggest lessons you learn come out of nearly missed opportunities? My schedule had been really busy with a lot of travelling, so when I finally got home I wasn't thrilled to hear that the next day was filled with one-on-one coaching. In fact, I was tempted to reschedule everyone, but the thought of letting someone down, someone who really needed a rewiring, stopped me. The third hour of my day made it all worthwhile.

I'd heard his name before. He was a moderately successful entrepreneur who, from a distance, seemed destined for great things. He was the sort of guy who solved other people's problems, yet rarely spoke about his own, so when he walked into my office he came across as being in control, but uncomfortable in the environment.

We chatted for a while and then I asked him how I could help. 'I don't seem to follow through on things,' he replied. 'I get things started, they look like being successful, and then I start something else. I end up with about a hundred almost successful projects, all of which I start with a passion, but then I lose motivation.'

I asked him, 'What would happen if you *did* follow through?' His answer came quickly: 'I might become successful.' 'And what would happen if you were successful?' He was visibly stunned by the answer that came to him. 'My friends might not like me.' He dug deeper. 'And I'd have to keep a hold on success, and that'd be a hassle.' In a very short time, we'd discovered why he wasn't following through: part of him believed that success would lead to pain. He feared success.

Our strongest instinct is for survival. If we avoid pain, we stay alive. The brain's primary function is to avoid pain. More than anything else, it will do anything to keep us away from pain.

Have you ever felt like there was a part of you holding you back? This might seem like a fuzzy sort of question, but it's actually not far from the truth of what happens. In my client's case, a huge part of him was striving for success. Most of him wanted it, but a part of him didn't. He would go after his goals with intensity, but then find a unique way to ensure he never got there. This is self-sabotage. Not only does this internal set-up make achieving hard work, if not impossible; it also makes happiness a rare experience, because two parts of us are in conflict and tearing us apart.

I was able to show my client how self-defeating his beliefs were and pull them back into alignment. He recognised that a friend who rejects him because of his success isn't the sort of friend he needs, and that being a success isn't nearly as much hassle as being a failure. At least if you have all the things success brings, you then have the choice to throw it all away if it's not what you really want.

Meeting this man opened my eyes to a principle I hadn't understood before: *We can only Happily Achieve when every part of us is aligned with and dedicated to our goal.*

I was first introduced to the idea of different parts of the brain when I looked into neurolinguistic programming. The developers of this system noticed that every part of our brain has its own function to perform and its own goals to meet.

I'll give you an example. Let's say that a part of you wants to keep you healthy, so you use exercise and diet as your strategy. But there's a part of you whose function is to make sure you have fun and enjoy yourself, and the way it does this is by drinking like a fish every second night. Obviously, this goes against the part that's trying to keep you healthy. Basically, if this was your set-up, there would be a small conflict looming. The night's partying would be enjoyed, but there'd always be a little guilt in the back of your mind. And look out if you didn't get up and exercise the next morning! The healthy part would be frustrated, and it would probably punish you with guilt and regret all day. Sound familiar?

What do you think happens if a part of you really wants to achieve in a big way, but there is also a powerful part of you that wants to avoid rejection at all costs? It makes it incredibly difficult to create massive achievement when that negative part of you constantly avoids situations and actions that might end in rejection. This is an unhappy achiever set-up.

~

TO HAPPILY ACHIEVE, ALL PARTS MUST BE IN UNISON.

~

I was fortunate to catch a TV special on Michael Flatley recently, the Irishman who has revolutionised dance theatre. Who would have thought that a dance show with a line-up of Irish folk dancers who don't move their arms could be so entertaining? Watching the performance, I was blown away by Flatley's presence on stage. In a group of thirty of forty dancers, he was an absolute stand-out.

When I saw a close-up of his face, I knew why. His expression told me that every part of him just loved performing. Not one part of him associated pain with what he was doing. In that moment, he had access to *all* his resources. Every single part of him wanted to be dancing at his best. It translated into the most energetic, entertaining and powerful dance performance I'd ever seen.

Fantastic performance, in any field, happens when every part of us wants what we are doing at that moment. I've felt this in my own sporting career. My last year was my worst year. There was a huge part of me that wanted to get its teeth into what I'm doing now. The last thing this part wanted to do was train and race in the ocean every day. For me, that was a waste of valuable energy. One day, I found myself in the middle of a four-hour endurance event, wondering about how happy the winner would be feeling. (Not an ideal racing strategy!) In the past, all my mental resources would have been occupied with finding a way to win. It was time for a career change.

Michael Flatley would perform poorly, or below his peak, if any part of him decided that what he was doing would lead to pain. For example, if the part of him that was most concerned about his health believed he was overdoing it and that another all-out performance could lead to a physical collapse, he probably wouldn't have a great show. This part might then use depression, or a niggling illness, in the hope that it could avoid the 'pain' of the performance. Of course, he would still go on. But he wouldn't be at his brilliant best.

When one considers world champion athletes, this principle becomes very clear. When they perform at their absolute optimum and break world records, every part of them is in alignment. All their mental resources are readily available to them. The same applies to massive financial achievers. Very few of these people would have any aspects of their character that would be opposed to making enormous sums of money. Their focus is uninterrupted, as they use all their mental resources to achieve their goals.

On the other hand, I've spoken to people who literally repel money. A part of them believes that 'money is the root of all evil', or 'money makes you greedy'. So, what does the brain do? It avoids money at all costs by developing a pattern of over-spending or financial stupidity to repel money, because for them, money will lead to pain. You might have heard the statistics on people who win large amounts of cash in the lottery — most winners end up in the same financial position they were in prior to their win, within a two-year time frame.

When every part of us is focused on the same goal, great achievements are possible. Happy Achievers are able to commit to an action with their entire soul. In contrast, the ineffective achiever says, 'Yes, absolutely, I'll do this. But what if it doesn't work? Maybe ... I don't know ... maybe not.' The happiest people in relationships are the ones who want to be in their relationship with all their heart, while the people who aren't as satisfied say, 'I like being in this relationship, but I wonder if there's something better out there ... I feel a little smothered.' Their dissatisfaction comes from their internal conflict.

~

HAPPY ACHIEVERS HAVE FEW INTERNAL CONFLICTS.

~

Keeping all our different parts in alignment is an ongoing process of negotiation. If part of us shies away from success, like the almost successful entrepreneur, we have to negotiate it back into line by helping it to understand that success won't mean pain, it will actually mean pleasure. We won't lose friends — in fact, it'll open the door to a whole new group of like-minded friends. Money isn't the root of all evil; it's actually the root of massive good deeds, because it's better to fight evil with good money, rather than no money. It's all a process of negotiation.

Try cutting deals with the various parts of you that are in conflict. For example, you could make a deal with the part of you that wants to exercise: 'If I promise that I'll exercise on Sunday, Monday, Tuesday and Thursday, will you let me sleep in on Saturday morning after a big night, without feeling guilty?' It sounds weird, but it works. However, if you *do* make a deal, you'd better stick to it, or be prepared for the part you've disappointed to make it even harder for you.

Your mind is your most powerful tool. Few scientists would dispute that the power and potential of the human brain is unlimited. In my experience, we get closest to full access to our brain's resources when every part of us is in alignment with, and working towards, the same goal. This is demonstrated by all kinds of achievers — athletes, artists and business people — every day. We see it in the extraordinary human feats we hear about every so often, such as people lifting cars off children trapped beneath, those who survive hellish periods at the mercy of the elements. Amazing things are possible when every part of us acts in unison and we become a united individual.

The bottom line is that we have to eliminate inner conflict if we are to be consistently happy and consistently successful. Any time you feel that things aren't in alignment, ask yourself:

~ **What is my goal?**

~ **Is there a part of me that's in conflict with my goal?**

~ **How can I negotiate with that part?**

PRINCIPLE FIVE

DEVELOP ABSOLUTE BELIEF

'Do you believe in God?' I asked.

'No,' he replied, without emotion. 'He has never revealed Himself to me, or given me any proof that He exists.'

I hadn't asked the question for religious reasons. I was sitting in the granny flat he rented, drinking a cup of tea, and as I glanced around I noticed that it didn't seem a priority for him to keep the place tidy. 'Maybe his eyesight's failing,' I thought, giving him the benefit of the doubt. The flat was tiny, consisting of three rooms: a kitchen/living room, a bedroom and a bathroom.

Our time together was usually spent talking of science and its applications. I was awed by his vast intelligence and command of language; he chose his words as if they were arrows and he an archer. I've often wondered whether he spent his spare time reading the dictionary. And it always made me smile to hear him speak with such modesty, as if everyone had his ease of understanding. His intelligence was as clear and sharp as it was unutilised.

This particular day, I went to see him with an agenda. I wanted to find out how a man with such outstanding credentials and blinding potential had ended up broke, unemployed and unhappy. How had he managed to fail? For a man with that much grey matter, failure is a difficult goal. Most people do well enough even without much conscious focus. For some, failure is as hard to achieve as success is for others.

His answer to the God question confirmed my suspicions, but I wanted to be completely sure. 'Tell me, do you believe in aliens?' 'There's no proof,' he shot back, as if I'd missed his point earlier. 'Science hasn't been able to prove their existence; it's only hearsay.'

I was beginning to understand the way his mind decided what it would and wouldn't believe. I asked a few more questions to see if his strategy was limited just to ideological topics. To my surprise, he applied the exact same method in every area of his life when deciding what, and what not, to believe. It was really sad. He wanted absolute and irrefutable proof before he could believe in *anything*.

A big piece of the puzzle dropped into place. It was great to have learned another valuable lesson, but at the same time I was saddened because my 'teacher' hadn't been able to escape from his own lack of faith. All I saw in his eyes now was unfulfilled potential, and there is nothing in the world that affects me as much.

~

WE MUST BE ABLE TO BELIEVE WITH OUR WHOLE HEART AND SOUL, EVEN WHEN THERE IS NO PROOF.

~

Happy Achievers have taught me that we've got to maintain our faith, even when all the available proof points in the other direction. If we are to go where no one else has gone, to do what no one else has done, to improve more than we ever felt was possible, we need to develop *absolute belief.*

Absolute belief enables us to keep believing when no one else does, when science says it's wrong, when our families and friends say it can't be done. It gives us the courage to stand alone, the only one left believing, if that's what it takes. Absolute belief is an essential part of any massive achievement, any outstanding breakthrough, or any occasion when the record books are rewritten.

The strategies we use to determine how and what we believe are mostly unconscious. We can end up limiting our potential without even being aware of it. One of the most common and dangerous belief strategies I've come across is the *past reference* strategy. I see it in athletes and business people every day.

It works like this: 'I won't believe something is possible if I haven't already done it in the past. I can't start a small business, because I've never run one. I can't win this race, because I've never won one. I can't write this story, because I've never written one.'

It may sound ridiculous, but we've all fallen into this trap from time to time. How often have you expected to have only limited success at something because you've never done it before? Now imagine approaching a new challenge from a different angle: 'I've seen it done well, so I know I'll do it well.' Or, 'I can imagine doing it well, so I know I'll do it well.' Have belief, even without proof.

The people I've noticed who are able to achieve their goals quickly are those who have an emotional state of certainty as a result of their belief. In this state, they have access to *all* their inner resources. That doesn't mean they can walk on to a tennis court and thrash Pete Sampras 6–0, 6–0, despite never having picked up a racquet before, but they'll take different actions and get different results compared to those who approach a task or challenge with uncertainty. Put simply, people who *believe* they can succeed tend very quickly to become good at almost anything they try.

The man who sat opposite me that day, sipping his tea, had failed to grasp that it was his customary thought patterns that stood between who he was and who he could have been.

It's amazing how resourceful we become when we really have the certainty to put ourselves in unfamiliar situations that have massive risks. If we approach life with absolute belief, we will try almost anything in order to achieve our goal, regardless of the risk or whether we've done it before. The result is that we learn incredibly quickly and achieve at great speed.

Let me just qualify what I'm saying here. I'm not suggesting that the goal is to put energy into a ridiculous belief in an absurd situation, like standing naked in the street and believing that no one will notice. I am saying that we are often unwilling to take the necessary action to go after our dreams because we listen to all of the bad news.

I hate to think about how many talented people would love to be actors but never pursue it because 'only ten per cent of actors earn a living'. This means that one in ten makes it work, which isn't bad odds when you consider that, by the law of averages, at least fifty per cent of those won't be doing what it takes to *make it happen*. They'll just be sitting around waiting for an acting career to *come to them*.

Absolute belief means keeping the faith, no matter what, and turning that faith into consistent, massive action directed at achieving your goal.

Another damaging past reference belief strategy is: 'I believe I'll get the same results as I have in the past. I've failed before, so I'm destined to fail again.' This is self-conditioning. The effects are seen really clearly in young athletes. For example, let's say that Jim was a late bloomer, so that at swimming training and in competitions he was always being beaten by the bigger boys in his age group. By the time he turns sixteen, he's caught up to the other guys physically, but *mentally* his past reference strategy has conditioned him to believe he is a fifth placegetter. When he races, everyone can see his potential — but somehow he never develops the will to win. Eventually, Jim gives swimming away, his potential untapped. People talk about having the will to win as if it were as rare as discovering gold in your backyard. Yet, it's in *all of us*.

~

THE WILL TO WIN IS THE BELIEF THAT YOU CAN.

~

We commonly use past reference when building our belief systems. Our mind attaches meaning to past events to help us be more effective in the future. The flaw in this system is that wrong meanings can be attached to events, unless we consciously control the process. For example, if a small business fails, its owner may subconsciously take this to mean that small businesses *can't* succeed. So, he says: 'Never again.' Yet, many small businesses *do* thrive, so maybe our small business owner would do better to take a more positive approach, such as: 'This one didn't work. I won't do it that way again.' Or, 'OK, it was in a bad location, but it'll work somewhere else.'

~

DON'T ALLOW WHAT'S HAPPENED IN THE PAST TO DICTATE YOUR FUTURE.

~

These days, a great deal of emphasis is put on experience. You have to be experienced to do this, or you've got to have experience to do that. To me, experience in itself can be as much a negative thing as a positive thing. When you hire someone with experience, you're also hiring their conditioned belief system — that is, their beliefs on how things should be done and on what's possible. Their past can work *for* you, but it can also work *against* you.

Sometimes, naivety is bliss. Because we haven't learned that it's impossible to do something, we do it anyway. And, to most people's surprise, we find a way to make it work, or we just plain get lucky because we've put ourselves in a situation and taken a gamble. Success is always possible if we take a chance.

Imagine that you had no past references to call on, to tell you if something is likely to succeed or fail. What actions would you take if you had no past? What would you be willing to try? Who would you be willing to speak to? Who would you approach with an idea? What new project would you start? What new concept would you pursue?

Given a little naivety and a sense of wonder, your dream can move from the impossible to the highly possible. Where could you be a year from now if you had absolute belief?

Absolute belief has been the trademark of history makers the world over. What proof did Nelson Mandela have that South Africa could be freed from apartheid? His faith was enough to sustain him for nearly thirty years behind bars. And did William Wallace have any proof that Scotland could be freed from the English? His absolute belief was strong enough to die for. If he had needed proof, he would have settled for farming instead of fighting.

Martin Luther King, Gandhi, Mother Theresa — all pursued their dreams without any proof of what the result might be. Walt Disney set out to build an enormous tribute to happiness and positivity. Dozens of bankers refused to fund it. Bankers aren't allowed just to have belief; they must have *proof*. Walt Disney had no proof, just absolute belief, and the conviction to turn his belief into action.

~

HAPPY ACHIEVERS HAVE VISION, AND THE COURAGE TO BACK THAT VISION WITH ABSOLUTE BELIEF.

~

My heart was heavy for the man I'd questioned in his granny flat. He'd never felt the passion of going after what he knew might be possible, and he'd never experienced the life force that courses through your body when the result is uncertain but you carry on regardless. He had only ever known sure things: that night will follow day, that rain is wet, and that light can travel a long way in a year. He hadn't learned, during his seventy-odd years, that what makes life really juicy is taking a chance on believing in things we can't yet see, hear or feel. It tore at my heart. When I left his flat, I promised myself I'd learn the lesson he had ignored:

~

TURN FEAR OF THE UNKNOWN INTO EXCITEMENT AT THE POTENTIAL.

~

Remember, it was one of the world's greatest scientists, Albert Einstein, who said: 'Imagination is more important than knowledge.'

PRINCIPLE SIX

DWELL ON THE EDGE

I often question whether the achievers have got it right. Are we missing the point? I wonder if the guy lazing on the beach on a remote island in the Pacific, without any possessions or responsibilities, has worked it out. I ask myself: What is the ultimate goal in life? Is it to achieve like mad? Is it to grow and develop as a human being? Is it to have fun, to enjoy every moment, forget about tomorrow and eliminate stress? If it is, then the guy on the beach really *has* worked it out.

I often find myself in a reflective mood. It's usually when my life isn't moving as fast as I'd like, or at those times when I feel that I'm trying to achieve against the flow. I know these periods are temporary, so I actually enjoy having the time to think. I also know there are no right or wrong answers to the questions I ask myself, but it feels good to ask them because it reminds me that no one has all the answers or the one truth. Nothing is right for everyone. In fact, the only thing that most people would agree on is that life is to be lived to the absolute maximum.

No matter what we choose, we must choose to do it with passion. In terms of the Happy Achiever's philosophy, this means always striving to move *closer to the edge*.

Have you ever noticed that the times when you feel most alive are also those times when you're experiencing pain and pleasure simultaneously? Achievement can be like that — although the risks are so great you can't sleep properly because your mind is constantly moving, you feel the most amazing excitement at the possibilities.

~

DWELLING ON THE EDGE IS KNOWING THAT YOU ARE ON THE RIGHT PATH TO DOING WHAT YOU LOVE TO DO.

~

I remember my first experience of being on the edge. He had sponsored me for several years as an ironman and I trusted him without question, so when he came to me with a proposal to work for his company in the off-season, I jumped at the chance.

The first few months were fine. The work was exciting, and the cheques were arriving on time — the perfect arrangement for an athlete between races. And then, one day, the cheque didn't arrive. I wasn't particularly worried, because after so many years my belief in him was absolute. A week later, though, I decided to call. 'A hitch with the bank,' he said. 'It'll be there soon.' I wasn't concerned, so I paid our suppliers out of my savings. I didn't want to sour our business relationship.

A few weeks went by and the cheque still hadn't arrived. Now I grew concerned. It's strange how years of trust erode in a moment when a person promises, then doesn't deliver. There were more phone calls, and more promises. I stopped paying the suppliers from my own pocket and postponed any future business, waiting for the money to arrive. It never did.

The phone rang for a long time, and I ran in from the yard to get it. As soon as I heard the tone in his voice, I started to feel sick. 'I'm insolvent.' I didn't need to hear any more — his debts wouldn't be honoured.

I sat on my bed, letting the news sink in. I did some quick accounting of the money I'd paid to keep the suppliers happy, and realised that blind trust and optimism may not have been an asset in this situation. By my reckoning, I had only enough money to last me six weeks. It would be twelve weeks before I'd race for prize money again, and another two weeks after that until I'd be paid. I had a huge problem.

I'd been gathering information from my interviews for years, but I hadn't set out to write a book. I had no idea what I'd do with the information, except learn how to be a more successful athlete. I spoke to Monique and we made a snap decision: I could make a few extra dollars by running a seminar in my home town, inviting everyone we knew. We didn't get bogged down in the pros and cons of the idea, because I'd learned from the achievers I'd spoken with that if you just commit to something, you'll find a way — particularly if it's likely to be painful if you fail!

Even so, I had to commit quickly before I found a good reason to pull out. Monique jumped in and booked the hall. Then I rang a few friends, the best gossips and the harshest critics. Word was guaranteed to get around, ensuring that if I bailed out I'd be tormented and laughed out of town. I was committed, and now I had two weeks to pull together two hours of material.

The moment we finished taking all the initial action, I felt a very strange and powerful sensation. It was a mixture of fear, doubt, anxiety, excitement, intensity, courage and determination, and I realised it came from *dwelling on the edge*.

For the first time, it sank in. To pull this off, I'd have to speak in front of over one hundred and fifty people — no small task considering that, at the time, the extent of my public speaking experience was talking to a class of school kids about surf safety.

I felt wired with excitement that I'd be able to express some of the ideas I'd learned from the interviews I'd done, and I felt alive in the knowledge that someone else could benefit from them. And for the first time, I felt another sensation. I felt that what I was about to do had meaning. My career as an athlete was all about me; but this was about other people, and it filled me with an incredible passion.

Which isn't to say I wasn't petrified at the same time. What if I made a fool of myself? What if I forgot everything I wanted to say? I had a mental picture of everyone laughing and walking out. What if everyone hated what I had to say? More images of people walking out plagued me. I had more doubts than ever. The worry and the fear was almost unbearable. Pleasure and pain at the same time — *the edge*.

As the date of the seminar grew closer, sleep became almost impossible. I'd wake in the middle of the night in a cold sweat. I dreaded waking, because I knew that I wouldn't get back to sleep. I'd leave the house at three in the morning and wander the streets, hoping to get the scary images out of my mind.

Why did I invite so many people? And why all my friends? It would be so much easier if they were all strangers. I was angry with myself for being so stupid . . . and so courageous. Damn interviews. Damn world champions. Damn achievers. I didn't know it at the time, but I was coming to understand the edge.

The night arrived more quickly than you can imagine. I look back at that presentation with a healthy level of embarrassment. I remember being so nervous that I yelled for the first half-hour. I over-compensated. I looked down and noticed people sitting bolt upright in their seats, almost fearful, so I toned it down a little. Two hours later the seminar was over. A few people walked up to the stage and thanked me — I think most of them were glad to give their ears a rest. But I'd had the *absolute best time.* I was hooked!

The next day, I got a call from a local businessman asking me to make a presentation to his team. I was in business.

I look back over all the things I've done and the decisions I've taken in my life and, without a doubt, deciding to run that seminar has had by far the biggest impact on me. No single action has helped me move faster towards what I really want. Holding that seminar taught me two of the most valuable lessons I've ever learned. First, *to really accelerate achievement, we must spend time on the edge.* And second, *life is at its juiciest on the edge.* It's no surprise, then, that I want to spend as much time as possible on the edge.

In subsequent interviews with massive achievers, I focused on the edge dwelling principle. How much time did they spend on the edge? How did it make them feel? The one thing that became apparent is that we've got to become accustomed to the feeling of being on the edge, because that's when we are really alive and achieving in the biggest leaps.

The edge is a place where life is uncertain, where the future isn't spelt out with guarantees. It's a place where our shortfalls are magnified a thousand times, where we are forced to improve so rapidly that *who we are* is constantly evolving.

When we dwell on the edge, things may not always work out, but just being there makes the possibility that they will all the more exciting. Even though we might feel massive pain, it's somehow justified by the potential of the result, and by the fact that we're taking the risk for a worthwhile cause.

Massive things happen when we are willing to step up to the edge. We must step up to the edge in order to fly. Unhappy achievers aren't willing to force themselves out to the edge; instead, they cling to the sanctuary of certainty.

Happy Achievers grow accustomed to the edge and learn to enjoy the feeling, to crave the uncertainty, knowing that if they are feeling like an edge dweller, then they are *right on track*. If they find that every day is mapped out and certain, and their time is filled with neutral emotions, then they take this as a signal to move closer to the edge. Happy Achievers live on the edge and sleep soundly at night, knowing that they are where they have to be if they are to achieve at maximum speed.

It's sometimes difficult to know what you need to do to inspire all those juicy emotions that go hand in hand with Happily Achieving. If you're having trouble finding the edge, ask yourself:

~ What action would I take now if I couldn't fail?

~ What is it going to cost me if I don't take action now?

~ What makes me feel alive?

~ What am I scared to try in going after my goals?

~ What am I really risking to achieve my goals?

BE CERTAIN OF THE SOLUTION

Knowledge is power. I don't know about you, but I've heard this from countless experts of one kind or another, I've heard people spouting it in movies and on TV, and I've read it in countless magazines, newspapers and books — and the thing that gets me every time is that it's glaringly incomplete.

We all know people who are knowledgeable failures. They *know everything*, but *do nothing*. In my experience, the difference between *knowing* something and having *learned* something is that *when you learn something, it turns into action.* Just knowing something isn't enough; knowledge can lie dormant forever. It's like water — it's good to know it's there, but unless it's tapped the crops don't grow.

The whole truth is much more exciting and so much more useful. Knowledge is useless unless it finds a way into our actions.

~

KNOWLEDGE, TOGETHER WITH ACTION, IS POWER.

~

Most people know exactly what to do. They know what it takes. They know the strategies that will help them to move in the direction they want to go. They've heard or read of the simple secrets for making it happen, and they already have the answers to most of their problems. The trouble is that most people don't *act on* what they know.

Risk-taking falls into this category. Everyone knows that they've got to take risks in order to achieve, and yet so few actually do it. The concept of risk is an interesting one for the mind to wrap itself around, because when we take a risk, we are doing the opposite of what our brain has conditioned us to do. Even though there is the potential for pain ahead, risk-taking requires that we push into that area. As the natural function of the brain is to do more to avoid pain than to move towards pleasure, risk creates internal tearing unlike any other. So, getting ourselves to take a risk is one thing. *Happily* taking a risk is quite another.

This word 'risk' cropped up in all my interviews. Any massive achiever I've spoken to has risked, and risked in a big way; at times, some have risked everything. I've always *known* this, but I got really excited when I realised that I was beginning to *learn* it, to really *feel* it. I was no longer satisfied unless there was an element of risk in my actions. Slowly but surely, it became encoded in my behaviour.

That was really inspiring until, after a while, I started to see the downside. I wasn't handling the risk very well. I wasn't happy. I felt stressed out the entire time. The uncertainty was killing me. I began wondering how massive achievers were able to consistently get themselves to take risks and, more than that, to be *happy* about doing so. Discovering a strategy for happily risking became the focus of my next few interviews.

Finding a happy risker was harder than I thought. Most of the people I talked to had a similar strategy to mine. They knew they had to take risks, but when they did so it was really stressful. In risk mode, we craved the security of knowing the outcome. When we knew the outcome, we craved risky action again. In other words, we were taking low-risk action, and for most of us that meant we were slipping into an unhappy loop — it was impossible to be happy, because when we had one we missed the other, and it's impossible to feel both simultaneously.

I remember thinking that this loop must be common. I spoke to a friend of mine around this time who was having constant problems with his girlfriend. When he was with her, he missed the thrill and the freshness of playing the field. But when he was single, he missed the closeness and warmth of being with his girlfriend. As a consequence, he tried to have both — playing the field, while not telling his girlfriend. Not a great strategy if you want peace of mind.

He was caught in an unhappy loop. He couldn't feel both of the emotions he craved, because in having one, he missed the other. The same is true for unhappy riskers: they want to gamble, but when they do so, they want peace and certainty.

A few months later, I found the man with the strategy I was after. During the week, I'd had several interviews with achievers who had done well financially. All of them were self-made millionaires. This man had one of the most beautiful houses I'd ever seen. The gardens were immaculate and the views breathtaking. He was dressed in an impressive suit — he looked like he'd stepped out of a GQ advertisement.

I was particularly excited about this interview because he was a true entrepreneur. His career had been varied, but he had been extremely successful in at least four different businesses. Each one had started out as a risky proposition. Many of the people I'd interviewed earlier in the week were quite conservative. This guy took risks. As he'd become more successful, the risk factor had grown; whereas most of the others seemed to get to a stage where they preferred to protect what they had, rather than go after something new.

All of this man's ventures had been initially tagged by the experts as being impossible, and at least three of them had never been done before — not in the way he did them, anyway.

'How do you handle everyone telling you there's no way you're going to pull something off?' I asked. 'I don't listen to all that,' he said. 'I just go in. It's when they tell you it can't be done that the biggest opportunities arise.' His voice was quiet and brimming with certainty. He didn't need to raise his voice to get attention. I got the feeling that when he spoke, people listened.

Later, I mentioned the project he was working on at the time. 'We've only just started, really. It's still at the risky stage.'

I saw my opening. 'When you're at that risky stage, how do you handle it?'

'What do you mean?' he asked.

'Do you sleep well at night? Do you get really stressed, or are you pretty relaxed with it?'

'To tell you the truth,' he said, 'it doesn't bother me too much. If you're going ahead with it, what good's worrying going to do?' That made sense, but it's a lot easier said than done. It's like telling someone who's about to jump out of a plane not to worry because they've got a parachute. There had to be more.

'So, even if things aren't going well, you rationalise that stressing won't help, so you don't stress?'

'Sort of,' he said, pondering his next thought. 'But there's more to it.'

I was glad to hear it, because I wasn't buying the 'stressing won't help' line. He went on: 'I just know that no matter what happens, I'll always find a solution.'

Every word struck me. His strategy started making complete sense. 'It's when things are really tough that we become our most resourceful. It's when we have our back to the wall and it seems like there's no way out, that we're at our best. I know I'll always find a solution, so I don't bother stressing. If things go wrong, I'll find a way to make them work. I've operated like this for as long as I can remember. Some nights I've woken up and started to worry, but then I think, "I'll find a way — I always do", and the worrying disappears.' He was one of a very rare breed; the happy risker.

The belief that he would always find a way had been the foundation on which he'd built his entire career. It had enabled him to continue starting new projects, go on risking, and live happily while doing it. He believed so completely that he would always find a solution, that he was never without one. He told me story after story about almost losing everything, only to find a way to make it work in the eleventh hour. Even in the most pressured situations, he could still be happy and keep the stress to a minimum.

~

BELIEFS ARE SELF-FULFILLING PROPHECIES.

~

I could feel his strategy taking hold in me. I knew that if he could do it, so could I. I realised that whenever things weren't going well, I never found the solution if I gave in to stress. In fact, it was usually when the situation got to a point so bad that it was beyond worry, that the answer came to me. It was as if the worrying was the very thing that stopped me from solving the problem. The mind can be so ineffective under stress, that finding solutions is almost impossible.

~

IN A STATE OF CERTAINTY, WE ACCESS THE MENTAL RESOURCES WE NEED TO SOLVE A PROBLEM.

~

Integrating this strategy increased the quality of my life immediately. When I found myself waking in the night and starting to stress, it would kick in: 'I'll find a solution — I always do. It's when my back is to the wall, that I'm at my most resourceful.' And, strangely enough, the answers always came.

I'll give you a simple example. A young girl studies hard for her exams and knows all the material. However, when it's finally time to sit the exam, she finds herself so wound up and stressed, she can't access the information. It's there in her head, but she just draws a blank. Then, when she gets home, her stress level comes down and all the answers come flooding back to her.

This strategy makes so much sense because, not only does it mean we can happily take risks, but it also means we have unlimited access to our own resources in solving problems. This is the principle of *solution certainty*.

~

IN A STATE OF ABSOLUTE CERTAINTY, WE WILL ALWAYS FIND THE ANSWERS WE NEED.

~

Try on the solution certainty principle. Sometimes, getting the feel of a new strategy is like trying on a new suit — it might fit straightaway, or it may need some adjustment. Being committed but flexible is an essential tool in Happily Achieving.

I know I've made a really big deal about risk, but it's so important in achieving anything of value. This doesn't mean that you should go to the casino and say, 'Andy said to take a risk, so I'll put the house on red 33.' What I *do* mean is that sometimes we have to let go of the things that make us comfortable, in order to go to the next level and create the sort of quality we're craving in our lives.

When we're risking, we feel alive. Don't allow yourself to fall into the trap of routine and normality. Dare to be different. Challenge yourself to be unique. Dare to go after what you really want. And, when you feel stressed about a situation, try believing:

~ **'I'll find a solution — I always do. It's when my back is to the wall, that I'm at my most resourceful.'**

PRINCIPLE EIGHT

GO FOR 'THE ZONE'

The alarm goes off way too early. Always too early. A lazy arm reaches out slowly from beneath the covers and the noise finally stops. She tries to sneak another five minutes' sleep, but it's useless. Her mind quickly fills with images of the boss with the attitude, the tantrums and the verballing, making sleep impossible. A picture of the next ten hours takes hold — so uninspiring. 'How long until I can take a holiday?' she thinks, as she drags herself out of bed for another day at work.

The shower is the signal to get moving, but the morning thought pattern continues, as it does every Monday to Friday. 'Why won't they let me run with my ideas? Why can't they see my potential? Just a few more years and I'll make the move.' But then she catches herself: 'I should be happy I've even got a job. There's so much unemployment. What if I couldn't pay my bills?'

Every Christmas she manages to get some distance from her work and to see more clearly. Every

Christmas she swears she'll take new action and go after something that will give her life some juice, something that will fulfil her. And each January she arrives back at work with every intention of resigning, but every year the same excuses convince her to settle for less: 'I'm earning good money. What if I can't find work? Maybe I'm not ready. There's too much at risk.' So, for another twelve long months, she compromises. But at least she's got the money and the security. Maybe next Christmas.

I know I paint a pretty ugly picture, but I'm particularly passionate about this issue because it's so important. There's a mind-set in Western society that has reached epidemic proportions. It says, 'I'm going to keep doing a job I hate, because it keeps me away from potential pain.' Or, in relationships, it says: 'Even though there's absolutely no electricity between us, I'm not going to change anything because it's too hard.'

Unfortunately, bad news sells. The world is becoming faster and more competitive, more companies seem to be downsizing, and unemployment figures get more publicity than Madonna. The bad news/good news ratio on TV is astonishing. It's so easy to believe there's more bad news than good. The way it's reported is completely off balance. We talk about ten per cent unemployment, instead of ninety per cent employment, and bankruptcy numbers rather than the number of business successes. The result is a society that will do almost anything to avoid the pain of uncertainty, of not having their futures mapped out.

In the nineties, security is 'in'. People will compromise just about anything to get it. I believe with all my heart that it's a global thought pattern we have to break. It's the compromise mind-set, or what I call the Level 4 mind-set. Our experience of life is a Level 4, instead of an *absolute maximum* Level 10, where we achieve better results and we achieve them faster.

~

HAPPILY ACHIEVING IS A COMMITMENT TO LEVEL 10.

~

The Zone — where life is lived at Level 10 — is probably the simplest principle in Happily Achieving, yet it's the easiest to break. The Zone simply says that *you must love what you do*. It says, the minute you settle for less, you lose. It's the anti-compromise principle. Life must be lived at Level 10.

It seems to me that, as the years go on, there are more unhappy and unfulfilled people than ever. My life's work is searching for the 'whys?' and finding the solutions, and the common factor in every unhappy person is that they have compromised themselves in some area. They have somehow managed to settle for less. It's universal.

So often, I hear: 'I'd leave, but the money's too good.' In an above-average life-span of ninety years, settling for even one year outside the Zone in your career is too long. Even if we create mega, mega, mega-bucks, we can't buy those years back. I can hear you saying, 'I have a family to support, and responsibilities.' But what is the cost to your spouse if you decide to settle for less? What is the cost to your kids? What lessons are you teaching them? It ensures that they will learn the same patterns.

What if, instead, through your behaviour, they learned to follow their hearts, live courageously and never compromise their dreams? That is true leadership. World leaders through time, from Braveheart William Wallace to Gandhi, are examples to us all that when you refuse to settle for less, your courage will conquer your fear.

The quickest way I know to be unfulfilled in life is to work in a profession that means nothing to you. Working in the Zone means finding a way to create meaning in what we do, finding something that contributes to the lives of others. If we want to Happily Achieve, we've got to find a purpose. Either we find a purpose in what we do, or we find something that does have a purpose. I can't stress this enough.

By the way, I'm not saying you should throw in the towel if you hate your job, and I'm not telling you to give in if things are painful. Even our Zone careers will be painful from time to time. We all have the power to make our present situation juicier if the job is what we really want. But, if it's beyond salvage, then get the %#$! out as fast as possible. Don't waste another minute. And if you're just starting out, it doesn't mean you should only settle for the managing director's chair. Cleaning toilets is in the Zone if it's a vehicle for achieving your dreams.

We can be happier only if we decide to follow what gives us the most joy and meaning. This will then have a massive impact on our career achievement.

Countless volumes of success-based material have been written over the years, but there is one simple rule that many writers have overlooked in their search for complicated answers: *If we want to achieve beyond our wildest dreams, we'd better be good at what we do.*

Getting good at what we do takes time. Time is the one currency we must invest in to excel. The trouble is, if we don't love what we do, we can't afford the time we spend doing it.

In my interviews and research, I've always found that the massive achiever's work is their play, and their play, their work. The line between the two is so fine, it may as well not be there. This means that they are in a state of achievement most of the time, to the point where often their challenge is just to switch off for a while.

People talk about needing discipline in order to achieve and succeed, but it's *not* about discipline. Discipline means you don't want to do it, but you'll do it anyway. Most massive achievers can't understand why achievement isn't easy for everyone. They love what they do so much, they do it without thought of motivation or discipline. Just let that sink in for a minute.

Imagine this: you're doing what you love to do. It's not a struggle to get out of bed in the morning. It's not a problem to stay late at night. You're even wondering whether you really want to take a break over Christmas ... It might sound strange, but it's absolutely real — the disappointment when the whole world shuts down over Christmas and you're forced to take a break. You're dying to stay focused, you love it so much. Everything I've learned tells me that if what you do seems like work, and every year all you're doing is hanging out for the break so that you can play, then the chances of massive achievement are minimal. You're not in the Zone. How different would you feel about your life if you loved your work so much you didn't even want to take a holiday?

Last night I surfed the net for a few hours and I came across the Married and Browsing chat line. It was sort of a weird way to pass the time, but I wanted to get a taste of the belief systems that would keep someone in a marriage that obviously had no spark. It was wild. I talked to men and women who knew their partners were playing around; others worked so much they only saw their spouse every lunar eclipse; or they'd fallen out of love, never been in love, or were in love but weren't loved in return.

I asked them all the same question: 'With life being so short, why would you settle for something that's so far below what's possible?' Their replies varied, but the underlying theme was the same. They all believed that the possibility of creating something special wasn't worth the uncertainty that would come with leaving. They all preferred to settle for the security — in other words, a Level 4 experience.

One woman wrote, 'The world is a tough place. I can't be assured of making money.' I replied, 'If it's money you want, money's easy. With so many people defeated before they try, there's no competition.' But the line must have dropped out, because I didn't hear from her again.

The bottom line is that the Zone principle applies to all areas. The minute we believe there is nothing better out there than a Level 4 experience, in any area of our lives, the belief becomes true. As soon as we believe it's too risky to try for something better, the belief becomes true. Start believing that something is impossible, and the belief will become true. It becomes true because we won't take action to prove it otherwise.

Going for the Zone is a lot easier said than done. Living in the Zone means doing the opposite of what Western society conditions us to do. It's about turning our back on security. The uncertainty is something we've got to become accustomed to if we are to Happily Achieve. It takes absolute courage to go for the Zone, and a belief that you're not willing to settle for anything less than a Level 10 experience in all areas of your life. The Zone is the essence of Happily Achieving.

This belief becomes a commitment to yourself that is so strong it generates every decision and every action. Designing your experience, your life, literally becomes more important than the global values of security and conformity.

~

COMMIT TO WHAT YOU LOVE. DON'T SETTLE FOR LESS.

~

So, now I need you to take your first step. Search your heart, and then — believing that, no matter what, you will make it happen — ask yourself:

~ What do I truly want to do?

PRINCIPLE NINE

PUT PLEASURE IN THE DRIVER'S SEAT

Tuesday.

'I want to quit. I'm sick of this sport. There's no way I'm going to win. They're going to have it all over me.'

If it had been any other athlete, I would've taken massive action to stop the decline right away, but I'd heard this before. She was in the top three in the world in her chosen sport and had a competition the next day. I looked at her and smiled.

'Since we've been working together, how many international competitions have you competed in?'

'I suppose about six.'

'And in that time, how many times have you wanted to quit?'

She looked away as she thought about her answer. Then she smiled sheepishly. 'About six.'

We both laughed and she started to see the strategy she'd put in place.

Thursday.

'We haven't started anything.' They shifted uncomfortably in their seats.

'Why?' I asked, feeling like a parent ticking off their kid for not tidying his room.

'We just don't seem to be motivated.'

At my first meeting with them a fortnight earlier, they'd been full of enthusiasm and excitement. Four business partners who, over the years, had created outstanding financial success. They had come to me because their business had lost its challenge for them, as it was running incredibly well and extremely profitably. However, they'd had a new vision. They'd barely been able to hold back their passion as they'd shared every minute detail with me.

Initially, my role was to understand their dream and ensure that each of them had a clear picture of the actions they needed to take to start building momentum. So, at the end of our first meeting, all four of them had very specific things to do before we were to meet again in two weeks. When they left, they'd felt pumped, like they were walking on air, ready to start the pursuit of the dream.

And then, the second meeting. 'It's proving really difficult to get started.'

I had a feeling about what was inhibiting their drive, so I questioned them a little further. 'What was happening at the times when you were at your most driven?'

They began to glow as they told me of the times when they were charging ahead at their best. Their spirits actually rose as they remembered being hocked to the hilt, with the bank breathing down their necks, and how the pressure of meeting those payments had driven them to take massive action and find internal resources they hadn't known they had.

The partners spoke of the periods when creditors would ring every day asking for their money, when a staff problem would force them to act immediately to avert a major drama within the business. As they talked, they began to see what was happening.

In the space of a week, I'd seen the same problem in two of my clients. Their strategies were simple: to get the level of intensity they needed to win, meet deadlines and compete at their best, they would have to be completely stressed out. Part of them believed that this would make them sharp, alert to all the possibilities, and therefore give them the best chance of winning. Basically, they believed that they needed to *hock themselves to the hilt emotionally*, to make absolutely certain they remained motivated. What they couldn't see was that it came at a cost.

As the partners began entertaining ways to heap more pressure on themselves, a new principle in Happily Achieving started to become clear: *they were all relying on pain as their motivator, rather than pleasure.*

Basically, there are two things that motivate people: pain and pleasure. Everything we do, every action we take, is designed either to bring us closer to one or to avoid the other. Some people will brush their teeth to avoid experiencing the pain of the dentist's drill or the embarrassment of being caught with spinach between their teeth. Others brush because they love the clean, fresh feeling and having sparkling, white, healthy teeth. There are people who will marry in order to avoid being lonely, while others are thrilled to commit to each other in such a romantic way.

The bottom line is that we either move away from pain, or we move towards pleasure, or we struggle to strike a balance between the two. What I saw in both my clients — the athlete and the businessmen — is that they had conditioned themselves to use pain as their *primary driver*.

The driver's seat principle says that to Happily Achieve, we must be moving *towards the pleasure of success*, not away from the pain of failure.

The athlete used the pain of failure as her motivator. In the week before competition, she would make failure such a real possibility in her mind, that it was debilitating. Her brain would respond by becoming incredibly resourceful in avoiding that pain and she would achieve a state of intensity strong enough to produce a great performance.

The partners had built a similar pattern. In the past, it was only when failure was literally knocking at their door that they were driven to take massive action. Their problem was that, now that they were comfortable, they had no reason to move.

'Comfortable', to my mind, can be a dangerous state of being. It's neither massive pain, nor massive pleasure. It's just a middle state, and it seems to be the state most people aim to achieve. To be consistently happy, we must feel that we are improving, moving forward and getting better at what we do. In pursuing and achieving our goals, we discover new inner resources and become clearer in ourselves.

The price, for my clients, of using pain as their driver was that reaching comfort led directly to stagnation. They had no way to get motivated if there wasn't any pain involved in the challenge.

I asked the athlete why she wanted to win an Olympic gold medal, and she replied that there were lots of reasons: the challenge, the success, the feeling she would have on the dais ... Basically, though, it came down to her wanting to win because it would make her feel happy.

'So really,' I said, 'your goal is to feel good?'

She thought about it for a moment. 'Yes.'

I'm constantly amazed by the psychology of achievement. We're desperate to achieve so that we can feel good. But we then take on a strategy aimed at achieving that good feeling *that makes us feel bad*.

~

HAPPY ACHIEVERS USE STRATEGIES THAT TAKE INTO ACCOUNT THAT THEIR GOAL IS TO BE HAPPY ALONG THE WAY.

~

The athlete's strategy for avoiding failure is successful if the goal is just to win medals. However, if her goal is to *happily* win medals, then the strategy is a failure. If she competes about twenty times a year, and she needs at least a couple of days of panic before every competition to fire up, that's forty miserable days a year, even before you take into account the natural ups and downs in the other areas of her life. Suddenly, having pain in the driver's seat becomes even more costly.

The same is true of the partners. During our first meeting, they had complained that since their business became successful, they weren't as happy. They had reached the position that so many people strive for — to feel comfortable — and yet it still wasn't fulfilling. Their strategy for achieving required pain as the driver, firing their moves forward. Along with the absence of pain there was an absence of motivation and personal growth, and so they lost the thing that kept them consistently happy.

~

ACHIEVEMENT IS THE TOOL THAT ALLOWS US TO CONSTANTLY DEVELOP.

~

One of the things I have noticed in massive achievers is that their achieving is consistent. It isn't subject to the same ebbs and flows as the average person experiences, where there are great patches of performance and then large lapses as the trivialities of life drag them back. Massive achievers achieve *constantly* — which means that, eventually, using pain as a driver will fail, because pain comes and goes; it isn't consistent. So, as my clients were finding out, with an unstable driver, they would get stuck.

I call this the journalist mind-set — nothing gets done unless there is a deadline; and even then, the deadline won't be met unless there is massive pain associated with missing it. The result is the division of life into two states of being — crisis and non-crisis — with very little in-between. Some people try to solve this problem by ensuring that their deadlines are back-to-back. However, the danger can then become that they get numbed to the pressure, resulting in the intensity of the potential pain needing to be that much greater.

As achievers chasing our dreams, we experience some of the most intense emotions — passion, courage, joy, pride — and they are addictive. We'll do almost anything to feel them. These feelings are why we want to achieve in the first place. But if we're using pain as a driver and we're not experiencing those feelings regularly, what will our brain do? It will ensure that we feel pain in order to push us into striving forward and achieving.

For years, the partners had focused on the growth and development of their business, to the point where it was producing beautifully. As the potential for failure diminished, so did the pain caused by fear of failure, along with their motivation and desire. Without the drive to keep them pushing ahead, all the juicy emotions they craved also disappeared.

As we talked during our second meeting, they told me that, for the first time in a long while, a few cracks had started to appear in the veneer of their business — not enough for them to get fired up — there wasn't enough pain yet — but the warning signs were there. They had taken their eyes off the ball for long enough that things would soon start to go wrong — there would soon be pain and they would be forced to act.

Using pain as a driver was creating a cycle where they would potentially sabotage their business, leaving themselves no choice but to access all the feelings they craved in order to save it. If we set it up in our mind that by succeeding we will lose all those feelings we love so much, then our brain can respond by saying, 'Let's find a way to stuff it up' — and losing motivation will do the job nicely.

The downside in conditioning ourselves in this way is huge because, at its base, it relies on us avoiding pain. People will stay in relationships that aren't right, because they want to avoid being alone; they'll continue in jobs they hate, because they want to avoid change; and they'll stop going after what they really want, in order to avoid the potential pain of failure.

What would happen if, instead of avoiding pain, we decided to move towards pleasure? What would happen if we decided to explore that new idea just because of the great feelings we'd experience if it worked out? What if we decided what we wanted in a relationship and didn't settle for less? What would happen if we actually did ask that person out and they turned out to be our soulmate? What if, instead of holding on tightly to that part of ourselves that might get hurt, we took a chance on creating what we really wanted, and risked our whole heart in love?

Happy Achievers aren't driven by fear; they are motivated by pleasure — pleasure in the journey, and in the success that follows. Happy Achievers are driven to achieve their goals by a passion for the pleasure of becoming the person they will be as a result of achieving those goals. Of course, there are still some fears and the potential for pain, but they are focused on the pleasure, so the potential pain isn't enough to turn them back. Their desire is consistent, because the primary desire to move forward is a natural state for all of us.

The only thing that even comes close to competing with, and disrupting this, is our desire to avoid pain. This doesn't mean that Happy Achievers don't listen to their fears, or let pain motivate them in certain areas from time to time, but the *avoidance of pain* isn't at the core of their actions. Pain isn't in their driving seats; it merely acts as a signal to show the quickest, juiciest route to their goal.

Happy Achievers approach challenges with an emotional intensity that is based on their desire to experience the pleasure that comes with working towards a great result and not knowing what that result will be, and in knowing that they are moving forward at their best, rather than being based simply on the desire to avoid failing.

Happy Achievers aren't emotionally hocked to the hilt. They don't need to stare pain in the face before they have the motivation to act. For them, achieving is based on the pleasure gained from exploring new ideas, from chasing their dreams, and from becoming the person they will become when they reach their goals.

In looking at why you are doing, or not doing, something, ask yourself:

~ **Am I motivated to be comfortable, or comfortably unmotivated?**

~ **What drives me to take action — potential pain or potential pleasure?**

~ **In moving towards my goals, are there parts of my journey that I can take more pleasure in?**

PRINCIPLE TEN

FOCUS ON BALANCE

Imagine if we were absolutely guaranteed to achieve our dreams. We wouldn't ever really have to worry about things working out, as determination, hard work and honesty would ensure success. Imagine knowing that, as sure as the sun comes up every morning, everything would work out. Wouldn't that just be ... totally dull? Pretty soon, we'd all be bored senseless. Although we crave certainty, if we actually had it, it would destroy us. On the other hand, never having a moment's certainty would be equally as destructive.

~

HAPPILY ACHIEVING IS ABOUT BALANCE.

~

Even positive things in too large a quantity can be destructive. Determination is a good example. It's common to see athletes who let their determination drive them into over-training and illness. Or business people who allow their determination to lead to family neglect and exhaustion. But what is a person without *any* determination?

The destructive power of too much love has been written about in history and literature throughout the ages — consider Samson and Delilah, or Romeo and Juliet. And we've all heard about the emerging phenomenon of stalking. *Everything is about balance. Good and bad in moderation.*

Health experts talk of the importance of water in the diet, yet I recently read about a woman in Australia with a psychological addiction to water. She is compelled to drink water all day, every day, and she is literally drinking herself to death.

What is the most positive thing you can think of? Laughter? We've all heard about the benefits of laughter, and yet even laughter could destroy. If you laughed for twenty-four hours a day you wouldn't be able to eat or drink; you'd even have difficulty in breathing. This is an extreme example, but it demonstrates that too much of *anything* is destructive.

~

MOST PROBLEMS IN LIFE CAN BE TRACED BACK TO AN IMBALANCE OF SOME KIND.

~

It's vital that we look at balance, but I'm bringing it to your attention knowing that I can't provide a 'fix all' solution, because there isn't one formula. The balance in each of our lives is going to be different. All I can do is give you a set of guidelines that will help you to find *your* balance. The other thing to remember is that any solution is evolutionary. As soon as you find an answer, another question pops up.

Finding a perfect balance is impossible; in a sense, aiming for perfection will push you further from it. Knowing and accepting that perfection is impossible allows us to see that developing a balance is about constant adjustment and focus, not a one-time 'fix all' solution. It allows us to grow, move forward and achieve.

Achieving some balance helps us to avoid the 'pain later' cycle. After years of imbalance, problems start to surface. A businessman who neglects his relationship with his wife while building his fortune is surprised when she suddenly leaves him. A teenager who spends all her time studying, finds when she leaves school that she hasn't made any close friends. The woman who dreams of becoming an artist but takes on a menial job just until there's enough money to start working on her dream, wakes up fifteen years later and realises that the job has become her life and that her dream is dead. The middle-aged man who has eaten badly for thirty years finds himself in line for heart bypass surgery ... It's an uplifting picture, isn't it?

~

IF WE ARE TO BE HAPPY AND CONSTANTLY ACHIEVE, WE MUST FOCUS ON BALANCE.

~

The key to keeping the balance is to become attuned to your pain. I know that this sounds very 'new age', but bear with me for a minute. Human evolution has designed pain as the clearest indicator that we are off-balance. When we're hungry, we need food to keep us going; if we're tired, we need to sleep; when our hand starts to burn, it's a signal to take it off the hot plate.

Pain is the fastest, most effective way our brain has of telling us that something's not right. When I use the word 'pain', I'm not just talking about the pain that makes us cry out. I mean *anything* that doesn't feel good. Stress doesn't feel good — it's a signal to take new action. Stress is pain. Pain is *any* emotion we don't enjoy or that is counter-productive.

The trouble is, we have grown accustomed to ignoring pain that isn't as immediately intense as physical pain. Emotional or mental pain is just as important a signal as physical pain. This is particularly apparent in our relationships. In my one-on-one work, I'm always seeing people who are experiencing some sort of pain associated with their relationships. Almost invariably, by the time they come to see me, things are on a downward slide and the pain is really deep.

A little while ago, I spent some time with a woman who had reached a state of what I'd call extreme pain. She could barely talk without bursting into tears. As it turned out, she'd been feeling this pain, though not as intensely, for years. Her relationship with her husband was now so far off-balance that her brain wasn't taking any chances — it was causing her *so much* pain that she *had* to listen. The bottom line was that she no longer loved her husband, and hadn't for years. The relationship was dead, but she'd done her best to ignore all the signals. She was now so unhappy, it was crippling her.

We must listen to the first signs of pain. Pain is a signal to adjust, develop or change something. The rising incidence of stress-related illness is a prime example. If a situation gets so bad that the stress is making someone sick, it indicates they have been ignoring all the earlier signals to adjust or change. In the end, their brain will manifest something so painful that they will have no choice but to face it. The brain is always striving to restore balance.

I see it often in athletes. They get so determined, so hungry for success, that they want to train every moment of the day, and they ignore the pain of injury. It seems obvious that if the body gets a cold, or a minor injury of some sort, it's a signal to rest. However, it's hard to rest when you're determined, so they train on relentlessly. Their brain is still trying to make them rest, so it throws a worse injury at them. If that's ignored, the brain gets really determined and knocks them down with something really nasty. This is true for anyone, no matter what their age or profession. Make no mistake, your brain will make you rest.

One of the most effective ways to test our personal balance is to look at the people closest to us, because if *we* are off-balance, then *their* pain is the easiest pain to miss. If our partner or our kids are frustrated that we don't spend enough time with them, it's a signal to take new action, to adjust and change. All too often, people lose what is most important to them by pursuing comparatively unimportant things.

~

LISTEN TO OUR OWN PAIN, AND THE PAIN OF THE PEOPLE WE LOVE.

~

Listening to the pain in our lives takes some practice. Society has taught us to ignore it. It has taught us to starve ourselves on diets, to accept depression as a fact of life, and to stay awake when we're tired, so that we don't miss anything. As a result, the signals get completely mixed up: people eat when they don't need food, they believe depression is a natural human condition, and they try to sleep when they're not tired. As long as we're willing to be patient and to develop it like any other skill, the brain will start sending accurate signals again, and our ability to listen to pain will become incredibly sharp. Pain is a signal to change. We must listen to it if we are to stay balanced.

Understanding the principle of balance is knowing that nothing is right all the time. No one type of food is right all the time, no one behaviour pattern and no single emotion. Even feeling down is right if it's balanced.

All of the principles in this book can only be effective when applied in a balanced way. What do you think would happen if you took the lighter side principle too far? Well, for a start, you'd lose all your friends, because when they came to you needing support, you'd just burst out laughing. And you would never take anything seriously enough to make the commitment required to see it through. Balance is essential.

As achievers, we are predisposed to become obsessive in what we are trying to achieve, and our health, relationships and families are likely to pay the price. We must be as focused on our balance, and on keeping that balance, as we are on actually achieving. In doing so, we guarantee Happy Achievement, and avoid the hollow victories of riding in that Ferrari with an empty passenger seat, cracking the champagne alone in our mansion, and watching our stocks rise from a hospital bed.

~

HAPPY ACHIEVING IS ABOUT FULFILMENT, AND FULFILMENT COMES FROM BALANCE.

~

To begin the process of learning to listen to pain, ask yourself:

~ **Am I feeling any sort of pain? (Stress? Sadness? Frustration? Anger? Depression?)**

~ **Is my body trying to signal me that something isn't right?**

~ **Are the people closest to me in pain?**

~ **What is the pain trying to tell me?**

~ **What do I need to change?**

BE TOTALLY HONEST WITH YOURSELF

I had one hour, and I was determined not to waste a second of it. 'What is it that you focus on? Is it the end result, or something else?'

'I'm sure people would think that I focus on the medals,' he replied.

He'd won many Olympic gold medals, making him arguably one of the most successful athletes in history. 'I try not to think about the end result at all. I rarely find myself thinking that far into the future.' He paused to choose his next words carefully, and my curiosity grew. 'If every day I can get a little faster, if every day I can get a little better as a human being, if every day I can just improve .01 per cent, then the gold medals will take care of themselves.'

Hearing this strategy from someone who was the *best ever* in his sport was truly inspiring. I walked from our meeting feeling that something I'd sensed for a while had become clear. It's what I call *primary focus* — that thing we focus on above all else. What I saw in this athlete was that his primary focus was *daily improvement*.

Having daily improvement as our primary focus can have a massive impact on our personal happiness and our ability to create momentum. I have spoken to people whose primary focus is the end result; others' primary focus might be failure, their personal shortcomings, or what other people might think of them. The choices are as varied as people are different. However, the advantage of having daily improvement as our primary focus is that it eliminates so many potential problems. It's what I call a clear strategy — one with very little downside.

During our interview I had asked him if he feared failure, and his reply had been clear and unwavering. 'I don't fear failure, because I'm not focused that far into the future.' It made perfect sense, because in order to fear failure we must shift our focus into the future and then envision a negative result. The athlete's primary focus kept him firmly planted in the present, where there is no fear about the future because he was absorbed in the process of creating it.

Using the end result as a primary focus produces two effects. When the end result is of primary importance, it puts enormous pressure on the need to perform, and few people have the internal set-up to be able to achieve great performances under these circumstances. With too much invested in the end result, we open ourselves up to frustration, fear and panic, three emotions that will slow our progress towards achieving our goals.

Second, the end result strategy pulls our focus from a concentration on the *now*. This translates as people not giving daily improvement the attention it requires if they are to sharpen their skills to the level at which they need to be in order to be the best at what they do. By spending too much time focusing on the end result, they neglect to do what it takes to create the result in the first place.

~

USING DAILY IMPROVEMENT AS OUR PRIMARY FOCUS IS THE MOST EFFECTIVE WAY TO PRODUCE RESULTS AND MAINTAIN THE EMOTIONS WE NEED TO BE HAPPY DOING IT.

~

If daily improvement is one of the simplest and most effective strategies in Happily Achieving, why do so few people use it? We lie to ourselves. We soften the truth. We fool ourselves about what our current situation really is. It's essential, if the daily improvement strategy is to be applied consistently, *that we be totally honest with ourselves*.

If I were to compile a personality profile of the type of reader who would buy this book, optimism would be one of the strongest traits on the list. If you weren't an optimist, you wouldn't believe that this book could do you any good, so you wouldn't have bought it. However, the danger with many optimists is that they judge themselves on what they see as their potential, rather than on what they are actually doing; on who they want to be, rather than on who they really are.

What would happen if you were courageous enough to be totally honest with yourself? What would happen if you were willing to drop all the facades we present to the outside world? Imagine examining how you behave every day, the way you treat people, the way you allocate your time to the things that are important to you, and being totally honest about who you are *right now*.

Imagine being totally honest about the things that scare you, about why you're not starting that project that you really love, about how many truly close friends you have who are really there for you, about the time you put into developing and maintaining your friendships.

What if you were totally honest about your relationships? How do you really feel about your partner, and how does your partner really feel about you? Imagine being honest about the level of intensity you have together. Imagine having the courage to be honest about why you didn't want to be in a relationship, or about why you're still in one that's not right. Could you be honest about other relationships — the level of respect you get from your workmates and whether they can rely on you?

Imagine if you were honest about your relationship with your kids and how much time you spend with them — and how much time they spend feeling disappointed with you. Take yourself back to the day they were born and remember the expectations you had of yourself as a parent, and dare to be honest with yourself about whether you're meeting them.

How honest with yourself are you about the state of your finances? How much debt do you actually have, and are you really servicing it? Imagine being honest about what you spend and what you save. So many optimists end up broke because they fall victim to the mentality that says, 'We can stretch it a little further. There's no need to save — there'll always be more money next year.'

~

THE OLDER WE GET, THE HARDER IT IS TO FIND THE COURAGE TO BE HONEST WITH OURSELVES.

~

The more we tell ourselves our little 'stories', the longer we make excuses for ourselves, the more entrenched they become. What if we judged ourselves on the results we are producing *now* – our financial position, our relationships, our job satisfaction?

If you've had three failed marriages, what's the one element in common? *You.* If friends continue drifting away, what is the common factor they are trying to avoid? *You.* It's too easy to pass the buck and lay the blame somewhere else. It's easier to believe the excuses we make for ourselves, than to have the courage to be totally honest with ourselves.

Total honesty doesn't mean beating ourselves up every time something goes wrong, and it doesn't mean over-dramatising a situation in order to punish ourselves. Adopting the 'I judge myself a thousand times more harshly than anyone else ever could' mind-set can be equally as damaging as deluding ourselves. Total honesty is making an objective appraisal based on all the information we have about who we are and where we're up to, rather than a biased appraisal based on who we'd like to be and where we dream of being.

So, why does the principle of total honesty have such an impact on daily improvement as our primary focus? Basically, it's impossible to improve at the fastest possible rate if we don't have an honest bearing on where we are to start with. For example, why would you apply your improvement focus to a failing relationship if you were fooling yourself that everything was fine? We've all seen the results — the broken-hearted lover, completely dumbfounded after their partner 'suddenly' leaves. Meanwhile, their friends aren't surprised at all, having seen it coming for a long time.

~

**TOTAL HONESTY CREATES A POWERFUL
DYNAMIC THAT ALLOWS US TO IDENTIFY
THE THINGS THAT AREN'T WORKING IN OUR
LIVES, AND THEN TO DIRECT OUR FULL
RESOURCES INTO FIXING THEM.**

~

Daily improvement relies on an ongoing process of being totally honest with ourselves, because as we improve in one area or meet a challenge, the balance is thrown out again. Total honesty allows us to constantly re-evaluate our strategies for achieving our goals.

The toughest problems to face are those that crop up after years of ignoring the signals. Total honesty means that problems are dealt with before they become crisis points. It provides a powerful base that enables us to be who we need to be to achieve our goals happily and in the shortest possible time.

I know that being totally honest with ourselves is probably the scariest thing we can do to improve our performance. We take great comfort in our excuses, because we think they will maintain our sense of security. It's an illusion — one that is more likely to create great uncertainty in our lives.

Imagine the other side. Imagine knowing exactly what you needed to take you to the next level. Imagine how clear the path to your goals would be with daily improvement as your primary focus. Imagine the power of honestly knowing who you are, where you are, and what you're doing, and the amazing strength that knowledge will give you on the journey to achieving your goals.

If you've just read this chapter without really asking yourself the tough questions, then I challenge you to:

~ **Have the courage to define who you are, and where you are in your life, RIGHT NOW.**

TAKE MASSIVE ACTION

When he walked into my office, I was astounded. The man I'd met years before had walked and talked with confidence, had been self-assured and centred. He'd had the presence of a motivated, balanced man in his mid-thirties who oozed success.

For many years, his business had powered. From modest beginnings it had grown into the model of an aggressive, exciting, rapidly expanding enterprise. Though probably too rapid. The years of growth had meant enormous capital outlay, borrowing that relied on similar growth levels over the following years. It was not to be.

The man I saw now was different in every respect. His posture was slouched and crumpled, and his eyes were fixed on the floor. Even when he actually managed to meet my eyes, the connection only lasted a millisecond before his eyes returned to the ground. As he greeted me his voice was barely audible, and it was almost painful to watch the hesitancy in his movement as he shuffled to a seat. Our communication during the first few minutes was obviously uncomfortable for him, to say the least. Every word seemed to hurt; every sentence was a real effort.

Although it was only small talk to begin with, just a way to get the ball rolling, his voice quavered and his eyes darted. He preferred silence. I realised that any contact with other people would be characterised by the same behaviour, the awkwardness and the uncertainty. Most of this man's time would be spent at home, alone.

I couldn't help feeling curious. What had happened to destroy this man? Surely a failed business couldn't perform so radical a transformation on such a confident, successful man? I was wrong. As I started to ask a few questions, his story slowly unfurled.

Yes, the business had failed, and yes, that had been upsetting. He explained that the first few months were the worst. His confidence had taken a severe beating, but he'd managed to pick himself up; he'd even started to feel like his old self again. He was doing odd jobs, nothing that required too much attention or intense focus, but then something had happened which reduced him to a shadow of the man he'd once been. He had woken late one night with an idea, a brilliant concept for a new business that he believed, deep in his soul, could succeed.

You're probably asking the same questions I asked myself: Where's the problem? Isn't having a great idea a positive thing? *He* couldn't understand it, either. How could having a great idea produce such a disastrous effect on him?

I asked a few more questions until I realised what had happened. The failure of his first business had caused him great pain. He felt embarrassed in front of his friends, and inside he was filled with more doubts than he'd ever had to deal with. His brain wanted to avoid feeling that pain again.

However, his ambition hadn't died with the business. In the back of his mind, he was plotting to create success in another business — *and here's where the trouble started*. He was wracked by internal conflict, because part of him wanted to go after his new idea with the same enthusiasm with which he'd started his failed business, but now he had to contend with a new part of himself, a powerful part that wanted to avoid the pain of failure at any cost.

The new part chose to avoid the potential pain of failing by preventing him from starting. The result? For the first time in his life, he couldn't get himself to take action. He was itching to go for it, but the thought of doing something about it was too frightening.

As we delved further into it, we discovered that during his entire life, he had equated lack of success with lack of action. Now, because he couldn't force himself to take action, he saw himself as a 'loser'.

And, of course, this belief was impacting on him in a huge way. It was eating away at his self-esteem.

I've come across this many times, but until now I hadn't seen the principle behind it. To Happily Achieve, *our level of action must equal, or exceed, our level of desire.*

Let me explain. The fact that you are this far into this book means that a big part of you wants to grow, achieve and improve. Knowing that part is there, it's probably fair to say that you're predisposed to feeling frustrated if things aren't moving in the direction you want them to. The trouble is, frustration, although admirable in a way because it is indicative of your desire and drive, is an emotion that destroys not only the journey towards achievement, but also the chance of achievement itself. It's just not a useful state of mind to live from.

It's hard not to get really frustrated when you're out chasing your goals and things aren't going well, but it's a thousand times more frustrating if the cause lies in our inability to get *ourselves* to act. We all go through times when our actions aren't quite as massive as they need to be, given the goals we've set ourselves, and during these periods frustration is usually only the first in a long line of dark, counter-productive emotions if we continue with low-level action.

~

SET HUGE GOALS, TAKE MASSIVE ACTION.

~

I've done some work with the long-term unemployed, and most say that they want to have a dream, just like anyone else. They start by going for a few jobs, taking massive action. However, the longer they go without finding a job, the more frustrated they get, and the more difficult it becomes to go to interviews because their brain is doing everything it can to avoid the pain caused by their feelings of rejection.

The frustration is intensified when they know they *should* take action, and don't. Now, though, the frustration is more damaging, because it's directed towards themselves. When they feel they just can't face going for it any more, their frustration turns to apathy, combined with a sense of low self-worth and low self-esteem.

The chances of someone getting a job while they are experiencing this internal turmoil are almost nonexistent, which compounds the problem further. Studying the physiology of the long-term unemployed has given me an insight into their emotional state. In a lot of cases they walk with a slouch, rarely make eye contact, and they speak hesitantly — an almost exact model of the man who'd walked into my office that day.

Frustration directed outward is dangerous, but frustration directed inward is catastrophic. When the dream is alive, there is a strong part of us that is unhappy if we're not moving towards it. If there's something stopping us from taking action, this part generates the sort of emotions often seen in the long-term unemployed. Such people have experienced that it can be intensely painful to have a dream.

The really sad solution which so many people choose is to put the dream away. Subconsciously, they decide to believe their dream is no longer possible. They choose to let the dream go, rather than experience all the painful emotions that result from not going after it.

When the goal vanishes, so does all the anguish and frustration. But along with those negative emotions go the juicy ones, too: the enthusiasm, the excitement, the passion, the courage associated with going after what you believe is important ... Gone. Life just got a whole lot less juicy.

The solution is to *take massive, massive, massive action*. As long as we are taking some action towards fulfilling our dream, the vicious cycle of pain is avoided.

Of course, there'll be some frustrations along the way, but not the type that cripples our character, or that causes the internal conflict that rips at our certainty and shreds our confidence, as with the man in my office or the long-term unemployed. They aren't the destructive frustrations that grow from our inability to get ourselves to take action. They are minor frustrations that won't eliminate the emotions we need to be consistently happy and always achieving.

There is no worse feeling than not being in control of ourselves, and the unhappiest people are those who feel that they can no longer control even themselves — the over-eaters, the drinkers who regularly over-indulge, the people with various dependencies. Their behaviour is controlling them, instead of the other way around. If action is needed, we need to be able to act, not struggle with it internally. We must know that we can get ourselves to do the things that need to be done if we are to Happily Achieve.

The simplest message to be taken from any massive achiever is that achievement won't happen *if we don't take massive action*. But it goes even further than that: *we won't be happy if our actions don't equal our desires.*

Have you ever found yourself watching TV when you knew you could be doing something infinitely more constructive? Many of the patterns we fall into on a day-to-day basis are like stealth habits — the ones that sneak in under the radar. We must monitor our behaviour. By continually questioning our habits and behaviours, we become more aware of what we're doing and why we're doing it. When our actions equal our dreams and ambitions, we can proceed at maximum speed towards our goals and eliminate the internal turmoil along the way. That's Happily Achieving.

~

WE MUST BE SURE THAT THE SUM OF OUR ACTIONS WILL CREATE WHAT WE DESIRE IN OUR LIVES.

~

Sometimes we may feel that we're giving it everything in going after our goals, until we take a good look at what's actually happening in our day. If you want a great way to shock yourself, send your mind back over the actions of the last week and ask yourself these questions:

~ **What did this do for me?**

~ **What is taking this action costing me every day?**

~ **What else can I do?**

~ **What more can I do if I'm really going to take massive action?**

~ **Do my actions equal my desires?**

PRINCIPLE THIRTEEN

BE FLEXIBLE ...
AND PERSISTENT

Her uncle had been relentless. It had started when she was eight and continued into her mid-teens. She had been subjected to a constant barrage of sexual aggression. Hers was a story filled with sorrow, but, as we talked, it was the conflict I could see raging within her that was most deeply affecting.

She wanted what most of us want: to fall in love with someone who would treat her with respect and honesty, someone whom she could trust and depend on — a man who would return her love with equal intensity. Basically, she wanted that 'spark'.

It's often useful to start by comparing someone's goal with their current situation, so I asked her if she was currently in a relationship. She said that she was.

'So, what's the difference between this person and the person you want to meet?'

She answered quickly: 'My boyfriend doesn't treat me with any respect. He sleeps around and flirts all the time. I just can't trust him.'

'So why are you still with him?'

She took a moment to answer. 'I'm just so attracted to him. I think I love him.'

'Do you *want* to love him?'

She replied firmly and without hesitation. 'No.'

She was experiencing an inner 'clash of the Titans'. Her relationship represents a problem I've seen in all areas of our lives, a problem that directly inhibits Happily Achieving. Her strategies to meet her *needs* were in conflict with her *wants*.

A *want* is a goal you are committed to creating in your life, while a *need* is a fundamental desire we all have — the desire for food and shelter, to be loved, to have fun and be stimulated by challenge and variety, and to move forward and grow through achieving those things that make us well-rounded individuals.

There are some very destructive dynamics at work when someone has the kind of experience this woman suffered at such a young age. Not only was she learning to read and write, and add and subtract, but she was also learning how to give love, how to receive love, who to trust, how to trust, and why. She was learning what produces pleasure and what will lead to pain.

Until recently, she had shouldered all the guilt and responsibility for what had happened. She believed she had let it happen because, although she'd hated every minute of it, part of her had felt special because such an important person as her uncle was paying her so much attention. She blamed herself, when, in reality, she was just a very confused, exploited little girl.

Imagine the results if her young mind had linked the abusive experiences involving her uncle with feeling special. What if it had happened during that period when her young mind was formulating strategies for how to meet her needs? What would the result be later in life, long after the memory of the conditioning had faded into her subconscious? Who would she be attracted to? What sort of partner would she *need*?

Not unexpectedly, she now found that she wasn't attracted to the men she *wanted*. She could only find the 'spark' with men who treated her badly, the sort of men she *needed*.

~

THE STRATEGIES WE USE TO SATISFY OUR NEEDS CAN INTERRUPT OUR MOMENTUM TOWARDS ACHIEVING OUR GOALS, OR WANTS.

~

You've probably experienced it yourself. Have you ever *wanted* to get fit, eat properly and stay healthy? At the same time, have you also felt a strong *need* to go out and let your hair down, to eat, drink and be merry? I came across a clear example of this recently. I was doing some work with a woman who *wanted* to get out more and to meet new people. She'd learned very early in life that the quickest, most effective way for her to connect with people and get their love was to get sick. When she was sick, everyone would call, or come around to visit and comfort her. This strategy had worked well for a while, until even her own family got fed up with the constant drama. Then, because her *need* wasn't being met, her brain's response was to make her even sicker, which only resulted in her being sick, alone and wondering why no one came around to visit her any more. Her strategy for fulfilling her *need* was sabotaging her movement towards achieving her goal.

We also see this happening in the corporate world. A woman might *want* a strong, happy family. However, she *needs* to ensure they are secure and well provided for, so she works long, hard hours that allow her very little time with them. Relationships become strained and there is unhappiness on both sides, pushing her goal that much further away.

On a personal level, a man might feel heartbroken because the woman he loves is drifting away, obviously threatening the fulfilment of his *need* to be loved. He *wants* to win her back, and the strategy he chooses is to cling jealously to her and constantly question her. The result is that she pulls even further away from him. His goal is in conflict with a questionable strategy aimed at meeting his needs.

We come across examples of this pattern every day — destructive strategies that have been conditioned into us long ago and which can end up costing us our goals — such as people who drink to feel confident, or take drugs to feel free. We all need to feel important, we all need to feel loved and connected to people, and we all need to feel understood and confident.

Destructive strategies all have healthy needs at their core. But how we choose to fulfil our *needs* will determine whether we can also achieve what we *want*.

~

HAPPY ACHIEVERS MINIMISE THE CONFLICT BETWEEN THE STRATEGIES THEY USE TO MEET THEIR NEEDS, AND THE MEANS BY WHICH THEY ACHIEVE WHAT THEY WANT.

~

Happy Achievers will go after what they want, while employing strategies to meet their needs that *actually accelerate the flow towards those goals*. Let's say you want to lose ten kilograms over three months. While this goal may also satisfy some needs, your need for fun and variety doesn't just disappear. Your challenge would then be to find a strategy to meet your need for fun and variety that also enhances your weight-loss goal.

Happy Achievers would ensure that the exercise they did over those few months was full of change and variety. Sometimes they'd exercise with other people, and they would choose a wide range of activities that went beyond just running and going to the gym — maybe rock climbing or body surfing, even sky diving — anything that would help them move towards that goal of losing weight while, at the same time, serving their need for fun and stimulation.

How many people do you know who set goals, but just can't follow through? In just about every case, some need has been ignored, forcing the brain to choose a strategy to meet it. The unhappy achiever would set a goal of losing ten kilograms and then choose a bland diet and a boring exercise program. After a few weeks, their brain would say, 'I need to have some fun. I know, let's go out eating and drinking.'

~

HAPPY ACHIEVERS DESIGN STRATEGIES THAT BOTH SUPPORT THEIR GOALS AND MEET THEIR NEEDS.

~

Questions, questions, questions are the key to this principle. In order for this principle to work for us, we have to apply one of the other principles, *getting conscious*. Happy Achievers constantly review the strategies they use to meet their needs. 'I know I need variety and fun in my life — is this the best strategy to get it?' 'I need confidence and some certainty in what I do — am I using the best strategy to make that happen?' 'I know I need to feel special, to make my mark, and to feel loved and connected — can my strategies get me there faster?'

By understanding our *needs*, and questioning the strategies we use to meet them, we can identify those strategies that may be slowing our momentum towards achieving what we *want*. Once we've isolated those strategies that aren't working for us, we have to search for replacement strategies that will fulfil our needs and, at the same time, support our goals. 'Are there other ways I could meet my needs that would actually help me pick up speed towards my goals? What are my other choices? Who could I talk to? Who already has the sort of results I'm hoping for?' Sometimes finding new strategies can be as simple as seeing examples of the results we want in the people around us and asking them a few questions about how they did things.

Finally, we have to test our new strategies. If you watch four hours of TV a night and you decide to find another way to relax, you'll soon know that the new strategy you're using isn't the most effective one if you still crave the TV.

~

EFFECTIVE STRATEGIES SHOULDN'T HAVE TO BE MAINTAINED BY RIGID DISCIPLINE.

~

It's very easy to get attached to our 'ways'. It's easy to justify our little routines — all those behaviours are just strategies to meet our needs. Happy Achievers have what I call *persistent flexibility*. They are *flexible* enough to search for effective replacements for the strategies that aren't working in their lives. And they are *persistent*, so that if the first replacement strategy doesn't work, they'll keep searching until they find one that does.

It's so easy to believe that the process of achieving our goals has to be hard, and that every step of the way is a new battle, but it doesn't have to be. It's a matter of freeing ourselves of the strategies that *make the process slow and hard*. If the road gets rough, don't question the viability of your goal or just accept that the way is meant to be difficult — instead, adjust your strategy. If you are persistent, but flexible, you'll uncover the momentum that will carry you towards achievement of your goals.

When looking at your needs and wants, ask yourself:

~ **What are my goals? What do I want?**

~ **Which strategies will best help me to fulfil my needs?**

~ **Which areas of my life are slowing me down?**

~ **Are any of my strategies undermining my dream?**

PRINCIPLE FOURTEEN

WIN NOW, WIN LATER

The camera followed him around the velodrome as he concluded his warm-up, the futuristic-looking bike adding to his already imposing presence. Four years' hard work had led to this moment, and the expectations were enormous. Although Australia is known as a sporting nation, our world champions come along only once in a while, so when an Olympic event featuring one of our rare gems was about to be televised, we as a nation were glued to our sets. He seemed to be taking it all in his stride. During interviews he was calm, relaxed and intensely focused. He was absolutely determined to bring home Atlanta gold.

At the start line, Shane Kelly's face was a study in concentration as he sat poised, his barely contained energy ready to explode. The cameras panned across the crowd, beaming the pictures of Shane's family and friends into our living rooms. There was a reporter on hand to catch the moment of victory with them *when* it happened. My attention was drawn by Shane's father. He was so focused, nervous and proud — all at the same time. He was on that bike with his son. As the starter raised his gun, we all held our breath in anticipation.

The start gun cracked, and our hearts bolted with excitement as he burst away. But then ... something so sickening ... He tried to regain his composure, but his foot had slipped off the pedal! His race was over in that instant — in a race that short, one mistake spells the end. His Olympic dream was in tatters. What was destined to be the high point of his life had turned into a nightmare.

The camera followed him around the velodrome, head down, obviously shaken and in shock. The crowd settled and fell silent. Shane's lap around the track took an eternity. How could this have happened?

Finally, the camera left Shane and found his father in the stand. Initially, he was stunned, and the reporter beside him was lost for words. Then, the shock dissolved into tears for both of them. I joined them. The entire Kelly family joined them. Australia joined them, empathising with a young man whose dreams lay shattered as a result of a shocking piece of bad luck.

When the emotion had lessened and I'd asked all the usual questions — How could life be so cruel? Why were things so unfair sometimes? What had he done to deserve this? — I realised it wasn't all that bad. After all, he was alive and the sun would rise on a new day tomorrow. It might take some time for Shane Kelly to come to terms with his crushing disappointment, but he would.

Having gained some distance from the initial shock, I now asked a new question: *What can this situation teach me?* I remembered something a friend had told me earlier in the year. When bushfires threatened many celebrities' homes in Malibu, in California, one technique used in fighting the fires was for helicopters to dump sea water on the flames. The helicopters would lower huge buckets into the ocean, scoop up thousands of litres of water, fly over the fires and then drop their loads. Apparently, when the fires were finally out and workers were cleaning up, they found two charred wetsuits cooked into the black earth. Talk about bad luck! Two divers minding their own business off the California coast were suddenly scooped from the sea and dumped on a raging inferno! I couldn't believe it. I was absolutely stunned.

When I thought about people whose lives are thrown off course by really bad lack, I couldn't escape the fact that *shit can just happen*. An athlete like Shane Kelly can be at his physical and mental peak, and be doing everything right — and shit can still happen.

Life isn't fair. It wasn't *meant* to be fair, so there's no point in *expecting* it to be fair. If life was fair, young kids wouldn't die of cancer, and people wouldn't be starving just because they happened to be born in the wrong place at the wrong time. A great way to be permanently disappointed is to expect life to be fair.

Perhaps most importantly, in terms of Happily Achieving, the shit happens factor (SHF) tells us that *our goals are beyond our control*. I can't tell you how many 'motivators' I've listened to who say we can control our goals and our results. It's simply not true. I'd love it if it *were* true! Life would be fair: if you worked hard, you'd always succeed. I know too many hard workers who are struggling financially; and I know a lot of hyper-motivated people who produce very average results. We all do. You can work very hard, prepare for every eventuality, be super-motivated — and shit can still happen. It may sound like a real downer, but acknowledging the SHF can actually be uplifting. It can help us to learn a lesson that would otherwise make Happily Achieving impossible.

Have you ever noticed how unhappy achievers tend to link pleasurable emotions to things outside their control? I'll give you an example. Many unhappy achievers make being respected by others a top priority in their life. It's one of the things that gives them the most pleasure. However, respect isn't something we can control. We can't force someone to respect us. We may behave in a way we believe will earn respect, but in the end it's up to the person giving it to decide. The person who craves the respect of others has no control over how this need is fulfilled. This creates a recipe for long-term pain.

Other people do the same thing with happiness. They believe they'll only be happy if someone does this, or another person does that; they literally give control of their happiness to others. To be consistently happy, we must not link our fulfilment to things we can't control.

All around us we hear comments like: 'I'll be happy when the government changes its position on small business.' 'My results will improve when the economy improves. No one's buying.' 'There's nothing to do in this town. The council should do something about it.' Sound familiar? This way of thinking prevents us from helping *ourselves*, or giving *ourselves* pleasure. It links *our happiness* to *outside forces* over which we have no control.

Another common mistake is to link our pleasure to the attainment of a particular goal or the achievement of a certain result. 'I'll be happy when the company can trade without debt.' 'I'll feel successful when I have a million in the bank, a house in Malibu, and a chateau in the south of France.' 'I'll feel confident when it's over and I've succeeded.' You can see how damaging this way of thinking can be.

Happy Achievers have taught us that we can't link our pleasurable emotions to the fulfilment of our goals, because, as the SHF reminds us, external outcomes are beyond our control.

~

Happy Achievers link their pleasurable emotions to things that are within their control.

~

The achiever we met in the introduction to this book had broken this rule. He had linked all his pleasurable emotions to the achievement of a financial goal. For years he'd said, 'I'll be happy when I've got heaps of money. I'll feel successful when I have the Ferrari.' His 'I'll be happy when ...' mindset ensured that he had experienced juicy emotions only rarely during the journey to reach his goal; and even on achieving his goal, he felt only massive, destructive disappointment. He arrived at the achievement of his goal and realised that he didn't feel happy, he didn't feel successful — and, as we saw, this left him feeling suicidal.

So, what's the answer?

~

Happily Achieving means linking our feelings of pleasure to the *ACTIONS* we take to fulfil our goal, not to the goal itself.

~

The only things we can control are the thoughts that we create and the actions we take as a result.

The consequences of those actions are beyond our control, so we must link pleasure to *action*, not to *results*.

A surprising number of people decide on a goal, then choose to work in a job they hate in order to achieve it, such as a salesman who sticks at his job in order to earn enough to feel free, successful and confident, when he absolutely hates selling. It isn't possible to Happily Achieve if you do what you hate in order to get what you want. We must link our pleasure to the *actions we take during the journey* towards creating what we want.

I wanted to find a strategy that would enable us to feel pleasure *now*, rather than one that adopted the 'pain now for pleasure later' mind-set. Considering how much we all want it, it's funny that something as straightforward as being happy can seem so complex and difficult. The simple truth is that *happy people make it easy for themselves to feel happy*.

A few years ago, I found myself feeling unhappy, and wondering why. So, I asked myself a useful question: 'What would have to happen for me to feel happy?' My answers really surprised me: 'I'll be happy when I win the series. I'll be happy when I finish the project. I'll be happy when I've got millions in the bank.' I couldn't help noticing that many of the criteria I was unconsciously using to measure my happiness were out of my control, and that made happiness almost impossible.

I decided to speak to a friend of mine who I knew was always happy. I asked her the same question

I'd put to myself. She replied, 'I'm happy because I'm alive. I'm happy because I love what I do. I love my family and I have great friends . . .' The list went on, but it really came down to this: *'I'm happy because I'm alive.'*

The reason *she* was happy and *I* wasn't, was clearly because we had set ourselves different criteria for finding happiness. Only when the criteria we use *are within our control* can we consistently feel the juicy emotions.

Do you think you'd take more action if you were achieving to be happy, or if you were Happily Achieving? Many people choose the first answer, because they believe that if they were already happy, they would no longer want to achieve. On the contrary, when we feel happy, we take more action, double our desire and really let go. When we feel pleasure, we want more. And how do we get it? By taking more action.

~

OUR CRITERIA FOR HAPPINESS MUST ALLOW US TO HAPPILY ACHIEVE, RATHER THAN ACHIEVE TO BE HAPPY.

~

Do you think you would take more action if you were achieving to succeed, or if you were successfully achieving? I can tell you, without a doubt, that the second is the most productive set-up. If you feel successful, you go for it. You feel confident about asking for what you want and about taking action and risks, to get it.

~

OUR CRITERIA FOR SUCCESS MUST ALLOW US TO SUCCESSFULLY ACHIEVE, RATHER THAN ACHIEVE TO BE SUCCESSFUL.

~

Many people wait until they've mastered something or achieved a goal before they feel confident, when, in fact, trying to master something or to achieve a goal without confidence makes it that much harder. If we're to tap our potential, we need to be self-confident. Why wait? Confidence is an emotion we can experience at any time if we decide to. So, make the decision to confidently achieve, rather than to achieve in order to feel confident.

If we are to be Happy Achievers, we have to make a commitment to spend our days feeling the juicy emotions. Making this commitment will have two effects. First, we'll WIN NOW, by experiencing the greatest emotions on the journey to achieving our goals. And we'll WIN LATER, by giving ourselves the best chance to achieve our goals in the fastest possible time. *Linking our juicy emotions to our actions, and to the things we can control, is the essence of Happily Achieving.*

When you're thinking about the goals you've set, ask yourself:

~ **Does my happiness rely on achieving my goal, or on taking action to achieve it?**

~ **Is my pleasure linked to the journey or the arrival?**

~ **Am I allowing myself to feel the juicy emotions now?**

~ **What has to happen for me to feel happy and successful?**

~ **Am I committed to WINNING NOW and WINNING LATER?**

KEEP IT SIMPLE

'Stop for a second. I want to ask this man if he wants a lift.'

I looked at Monique, and she knew what I was thinking before I had a chance to open my mouth. We were in a hurry. Monique went on: 'Look at him limping. He can barely walk. We should give him a lift to where he's going.'

'What if he's on his way to Darwin?' I muttered as I reluctantly pulled off to the side of the road. Monique jumped out and ran over to the man. He was dressed in an old singlet, a pair of stubbie shorts that had seen better days, and a pair of thongs. He was about forty-five, and unkempt — profoundly unkempt in a way that said it wasn't just a bad day. Life had beaten this man down.

I could see him shaking his head as Monique offered him a lift. I got the impression he was turning down her offer not because he didn't want a lift, but because he felt uncomfortable about inconveniencing a perfect stranger. But Monique wasn't taking 'no' for an answer and within a minute they were heading slowly towards the car. It wasn't until he got closer that I could see the pain etched on his face. He started to protest again, but Monique reassured him and told him not to be silly. 'We didn't have anything to do today anyway.' I just smiled.

As Monique helped our new friend into the front passenger seat, I smelled the alcohol. He hadn't been drinking that day, but he'd certainly given it a strong nudge the night before. While Monique closed his door and hopped into the back, I glanced down at his feet; they were shiny red and badly swollen, and looked incredibly painful.

'I've just been to the doctor. He says I'll have to stay off the pegs for a few days,' he said, trying to break the ice. 'He said I have a few problems down there.' Another quick glance at his feet told me that 'a few problems' was probably the understatement of the year. He had the worst case of gout I'd ever seen.

I asked him where he was going and he said he was on his way to the chemist to get a prescription filled, and then he was going to walk home. 'None of my family and friends live around here, and I don't have a car. I'd really like to thank you for your kindness.' He wasn't looking for sympathy; he was just relieved and very appreciative. I couldn't help feeling a little guilty about my initial reluctance to get involved. Monique could tell I was softening.

It wasn't long before the chemist had filled his prescription and within twenty minutes we were parked outside the man's house. He'd talked from the time he got into the car until we got home — about his family, the hard times, and the reasons he was down on his luck. The more he talked, the worse I felt about my earlier reaction to Monique's suggestion that we help him out. I couldn't believe that I'd been so heartless and selfish, that I'd been so willing to put a few unimportant tasks ahead of this man's obvious need.

'I can't thank you enough. It's not often that people go out of their way like this. It's good to know there are still some nice people in the world. It gives you hope.' He turned abruptly as his eyes started to water. 'Maybe I'll see you again some time.' He stepped out of the car and stumbled off towards his front door, and we drove away.

After a while I looked at Monique and she could tell that I was doing some serious soul-searching. I was ashamed. I'd devoted my life to finding the answers that I hoped would help people, and yet I'd gotten it so wrong with someone who really was in need. I sit in interview after interview searching for complicated solutions and strategies. How does he arrange his mind to win? What does he focus on? What picture is he forming? Which beliefs does he rely on? What's the source of his emotional states? Sometimes I get it so wrong.

In the closing years of the twentieth century we seem to have adopted a mind-set that says, 'If it's simple, it isn't worth much.' We crave complicated answers — the more complicated they are, the more effective they must be. The more complicated an answer, the more chance it's right. My experience with my new friend told me something different: *the most powerful path in life is the simple path*.

Monique lives her life according to one of the simplest — and yet rarest — personal codes around: *be nice to people*. Imagine what the world would be like if everyone lived their life according to such simple principles. Imagine what *your* world would be like if *you* decided to take on board some simple truths.

~

ACTING ACCORDING TO SIMPLE PRINCIPLES CAN ELEVATE OUR LIVES, AND THE LIVES OF PEOPLE AROUND US, TO NEW LEVELS.

~

How would our lives change if we began living according to a few simple truths? Let's look at a number of these.

Nothing is more important than my health

Most people understand and believe in this concept, but how many actually practise it? If you accept it as a personal standard, it means that you value energy. To gain maximum momentum, we have to maximise our energy levels. As achievers, in looking for new strategies, more knowledge, the leading technology, anything that will get us closer to the edge, we often overlook the simple things that are most important, like having the energy to maintain our drive forward.

Imagine how much more you could experience in life if you had more energy. Imagine the clarity of thought and the creative intensity you'd have if you had the energy to hold your focus for twice as long, with fewer breaks. If you acted as if your health really *was* more important than even your family, I wonder if you'd then find that you had more time and energy for them. If you decided to live according to this simple idea, I wonder how many other areas of your life would change.

I do what I say I'm going to do

Does this describe the way you live? If you make a promise, you deliver. If you say you'll return a call, you return it. If you say that you'll take your kids to the park, you take them. If you say that your partner is the most important thing in your life, then your actions reflect this. If you say you'll be there, then you *are* there.

Imagine how the people around you would feel if they didn't have to second guess you all the time, if they always knew where they stood with you. Imagine how much trust would flow through to you if people believed they could always rely on you.

Imagine how much your inner certainty would grow if you knew that you had kept a promise you'd made to yourself. Imagine putting yourself first for a while and having it translate into your actions. How much would your confidence improve if you trusted yourself to follow through? It's a simple concept, but has potentially powerful effects.

I don't worry about the things I can't control

If you walked away from this book with nothing else but a commitment to this idea, then I'd be happy. Living this simple concept means that we don't worry about what people think about us, we don't worry about the results if we're properly prepared, we don't worry about the past, the future, the weather or meteorites. Actively applying this simple idea eliminates many of the elements that can potentially inhibit the resourceful emotional states that make our life juicy.

I follow my heart

This concept is so simple that it's almost considered a joke, yet it's one that separates a happy life from a sad one. What would happen to you if, instead of listening to that part of yourself that's afraid, the part that wants to conform, the part that has doubts, you listened instead to your heart and had the courage to act on it? What action would you take if you let this simple idea permeate into every area of your life? If it was more important to follow your heart than to remain comfortable and secure, what would you do? Who would you be with? Which profession would you be in?

You're probably asking yourself, 'How do I know what my heart's saying?', because sometimes it feels like we've got ten hearts saying ten different things. The answer is simple. Listening to your heart is like building a muscle — the more you use it, the stronger it gets. The trouble is, we've become so used to listening to so many other things that the signal has become weak. History has shown that the people who have shaped our world, who have stood out in some positive way, have followed their heart.

Be happy

This idea couldn't be simpler: *we can just decide to be happy*. We can decide to feel the emotion. We don't have to wait until we're millionaires, until we meet the partner we've been searching for, or until we have more friends than we can keep up with. Living this idea means that we don't settle for road rage, we don't discipline our kids from a place of anger, we don't hold on to hurt or grudges for years, and we don't allow other people to control our emotional states. Inherent in this concept is the understanding that we can *choose*. If being happy is a motivating force in our lives, we can simply exercise the power of choice — the choice to be happy, regardless of the emotions created by a particular environment.

I do what I think is right

Imagine if you approached every decision with curiosity, and then had the internal fortitude to ignore all the social pressures that can pull you from your purpose and just do what you think is right. I believe that the number one quality of all true leaders is their ability to stand up and do what they think is right. Few people can do it. Imagine the power that would come from being able to live according to this simple code. Imagine how you would feel knowing that you were strong enough in your belief about what's right to weather any test.

How many of us actually apply these simple but effective codes to our lives? The reality is that most people don't let their knowledge translate into action — and don't think I'm excluding myself here. The chances are that you've read plenty of material designed to make you better at what you do and a better person. Some of it will have been good and some of it will have been bad, but the question remains: How much of it are you living? How much have you translated into action? Are you happy with the level at which you're living your life?

A large percentage of self-development junkies never improve their lives, despite going to all the seminars, reading all the books and listening to all the tapes. The only thing that improves is their emotional state while they're watching, reading and listening.

There is no lasting change, *because they never apply the knowledge they have received*. This simple mistake leads them to believe that change isn't possible because, despite all they've done, nothing has changed for them.

~

SIMPLE IDEAS AREN'T LACKING, SIMPLE APPLICATION IS.

~

One reason that we search for complicated solutions is that, although we basically agree with the simple answers, *they're not sexy enough*. We feel there has to be something a little more flashy that will get us there faster. But instead of filling our heads with more and more complicated ideas, I wonder what would happen if we confined our focus to one or two simple ideas; then, once we'd mastered them, we could focus on one or two more ideas. What would happen if we chose to adopt 'keep it simple' as a strategy? The reason so many of us don't improve at the rate we'd like to is that we try to improve too many things at once, diluting our focus and limiting our prospects.

By focusing on a few simple strategies that can have a great impact on our lives, we can create the best opportunities for improvement. It's so easy to turn being happy or achieving our goals into a complicated mass of ideas that only serves to confuse us more, when all we really need to do is acknowledge and live according to some simple truths that we already know in our hearts. Happily Achieving is about improving, and keeping things simple is at the heart of continual improvement.

~ **Which areas of my life seem difficult and complicated?**

~ **Why are they complicated?**

~ **What simple principles do I need to apply?**

~ **What are the clearest paths to my goals?**

PRINCIPLE SIXTEEN

CLOSE THE GAP

The ironman scene can be pretty cliquey. For example, there's the 'serious' clique — the guys who do everything right, completely by the book. They're totally committed; they eat the right foods, train the right number of hours and generally live the life of an athlete. A night out is a once-a-year treat. Occasionally, they might go to a movie, but generally, they prefer to sleep. I once shared a room with one of the most serious of these guys, and before bed each night he'd go through a full exercise routine that lasted almost an hour.

This routine took him all around the room in his search for the best places to stretch. At one stage I watched in astonishment as he spent five minutes in the wardrobe stretching his shoulders. Each morning I was woken at 4 a.m. by the noise of his screeching juicer, as he was in the habit of drinking his carrot and beetroot juice before sunrise.

Every hour of every day somehow slotted into the routine. I finally had to say something when I saw him tucking his singlet into his boxer shorts as he got ready for bed. 'Do you think it'll stay tucked in all night?' I asked. 'Just a habit,' he replied unconcerned.

The serious guys might have a lot of strange rituals, but they're some of the best athletes. There's also the 'silent' clique, made up of quiet, shy, unassuming guys. They tend to stay on the outskirts, where they're almost invisible. We would be away racing for a week and only see them a couple of times. If they were around, they'd rarely talk, which made getting to know them a challenge. Every now and then, they'd come out of their shell, but most of the time they kept to themselves.

And then there's the 'cool' clique. In the early days, most of the best athletes were in this group. These guys would race hard and play hard. It was just as important to be at the nightclub as it was to be on the starting line, and the competition for girls was just as ferocious as it was for the prize at the end of a race. These guys had fun, and their attitude said it all: 'It's a shame these races are interrupting our partying.'

As most of the personalities in the group were famous, everywhere they went they pulled a crowd. The guys didn't waste a second. Insiders were always amazed by their racing and partying experiences. I'd hear the stories in our hotel corridors: 'I was out with him till three o'clock last night and he must've had fifteen beers ... and he *still* won!' They were legends, especially to the younger athletes.

Finally, there are always a few competitors who don't really fit into any clique. They're friends with members of the other cliques, but aren't committed to any particular one. They tend to spend a fair amount of time alone. By the end of my career as an ironman, I was one of them. But it hadn't always been that way.

I was eighteen when I first joined the ironman series. I'd been watching it on TV for years, so for the first few races I was totally star-struck. I was so excited to see my idols up close for the first time. It didn't take me long, though, to work out who was who, and what was what, and I fitted nicely into the 'silent' clique.

However, during my second season I started to gain in confidence. I was now on a first name basis with all my idols, and I'd heard all the stories about the girls, the parties, the fun, and about the status that comes with winning races. I decided I wanted to be in the 'cool' clique. I wanted it more than anything.

I started hanging out with the cool guys sometimes — not really on the inside, more on the fringes. I wasn't making the plays, but I was participating in them. I'd go out with the guys at night, drink heaps and party. I was known as a 'kid' with a lot of potential, so they didn't mind me being around. This went on for the whole summer, but it wasn't until after the racing season that I started noticing the effects.

As a teenager I was pretty confident. I knew who I was and what I wanted to achieve. I remember going to a sports psychologist and filling out a personality questionnaire. When he came back into the room after studying the results, he said: 'Well, you haven't got an insecurity problem.' I'd scored the highest results he'd ever seen in the self-esteem section of the test. I thought, 'What the hell's self-esteem?' But he seemed impressed, so I didn't ask.

I returned home after that 'cool' summer, feeling emotions that were completely unfamiliar to me: hesitation, confusion. I'd never experienced so many doubts and insecurities. For the first time in my life, I was feeling self-conscious. The people closest to me picked it up, but it took me a few months to work out what had actually happened.

The main thing I noticed during those few months was that I'd started to question my every behaviour. Before I'd say anything, I'd ask myself: 'Should I say this? Will I look like an idiot? Is this the right thing to say?' The doubts kept coming, and they weren't just confined to what I said. I'd second guess my actions, too. 'Should I do this? Is this a "cool" thing to do? What will other people think?' There was no longer any certainty in my thoughts or my actions. Before that summer, I'd known exactly who I was. Suddenly I wasn't so sure, and I really needed to know why.

Trying to be accepted into this new clique had been disastrous for my internal set-up. I was trying so hard that I was losing who I was. I was turning myself inside-out to be the person I thought they wanted me to be, because I was sure the real me wouldn't fit in very well. I was right. When I was around those guys, I'd hear myself saying things I wouldn't normally say and doing things I wouldn't normally do. Because I wasn't being myself, I'd have to think carefully about my every move. 'How should I act here? What should I do?'

I was hesitating, no longer just doing what came naturally. Because I now had to plot everything first, this left me in a permanent state of confusion and self-consciousness. I realised there was a gap between *who I was* and *how I wanted to be perceived*. I was caught in the gap between the reality and the perception.

For as long as I've had the passion for Happily Achieving, I've wondered why so many high-profile achievers seem to end up in destructive loops. Marilyn Monroe, Elvis Presley, Janis Joplin, Kurt Cobain, Jim Morrison, Jimi Hendrix ... Just when they seemed to have it all, they indulged in behaviours that caused them to self-destruct. One day, during a seminar, I made the connection.

I was interviewing one of the country's leading marathon runners. His belief systems had obviously helped him to create some fantastic achievements. In closing, I asked him a question that, to be honest, was for my own benefit: 'Why do you think so many high-profile athletes are so unhappy?' His reply was thoughtful and concise. 'It's easy to believe your own press and forget who you are. People can get down on themselves when they don't feel they can live up to the public perception.' That's when I really saw and understood the gap between reality and perception, between who we really are and who we're perceived to be.

The effects of this destructive gap on outstanding achievers became really clear. What happens when the gap becomes so wide that it's impossible to live up to the perception? What happens when the perception is God-like? What happens when you're Elvis? Initially, the drugs are a way to become someone different, someone who's confident and feels secure. However, soon they're the only means to meet the public's perceptions, and living without them makes the gap too wide.

What can we learn from high-profile unhappy achievers? First, they show graphically that achievement doesn't guarantee happiness. And second, because they're in the public eye, we get an idea of who they are by the actions they take, and so it's easier to see the pitfalls of the gap by the mistakes they make.

We can't generalise about the cause of any particular behaviour, because it will be different in each of us, but I've noticed that the gap between our reality and other people's perception of us is the root of many unhappy thought and behavioural patterns. We all fall into the gap now and then. Sometimes, we don't feel like our usual selves at work, or when we meet people for the first time, or when we spend time with a certain group of people; but if we're going to Happily Achieve and enjoy the spoils of our success, we must constantly strive to *close the gap*.

It's interesting how some of the most valuable answers come when you least expect them. I wanted to find a strategy for closing the gap and keeping it closed, and I found it by studying something completely different.

Over the course of a few weeks I'd grown increasingly curious about something I call *silent power*. I'd first come across it at a dinner function. A man I'd never met walked into the room and I was immediately struck by his presence. There was something about him. In a room full of high achievers, he stood out. He wasn't doing anything out of the ordinary — it just happened.

I glanced around the room and realised that other people were noticing him, too. He wasn't famous, but there was something special about him that had nothing to do with the things that normally account for presence. It was the way he held himself, the way he walked, the look on his face — it was a combination of many things. I couldn't put my finger on it, until I realised that what he had was silent power.

I spoke to a few of my friends later in the week, wondering if they'd ever noticed anyone who had this kind of power. 'Sure, a woman I met six months ago had this aura about her of being someone really special,' said one. 'A friend of my dad has real "presence". I can't explain it,' said another. Everyone had experienced what I'd experienced, but I couldn't stop thinking about it. I was overwhelmed with curiosity about what created silent power. I had to find out, so I made a commitment to myself that when I next noticed someone with that presence, I'd talk to them and find out where it came from.

Over the next few months I kept my eye out at conferences, seminars, dinners and events everywhere I went, and over time I came across a handful of people who had IT. Each time, I tried to strike up a conversation. Sometimes it came to nothing, but what I learned from the others made it all worthwhile.

They were all very different people, with their own way of going about things, but one thing held true for all of them: *being accepted wasn't important to them.* They each explained it differently, but basically their bottom line was: 'I am what I am, and I do what I do.' This way of thinking gave them certainty in any situation. Because they didn't need other people's approval, they weren't trying to win any popularity contests; as a result, people were drawn to them.

~

HAPPY ACHIEVERS ARE WHAT THEY ARE, AND DO WHAT THEY DO.

~

However, the most important result of this strategy was that it completely eliminated the gap between their reality and how they are perceived. Regardless of the situation, people with silent power are *always* themselves, because they don't have any need to control others' perceptions of them.

The interesting thing I noticed in talking to people who had silent power was how easy and relaxed the conversations were. It was like their certainty soaked into the people they spoke to, unlike those stilted conversations we've all had with someone who's uncomfortable in themselves and obviously too concerned about what we think. I remember having done the same thing, trying to say what the person wanted to hear, rather than what I really thought. It's awkward and it only serves to drain our confidence.

The achievers with silent power are special because they've managed to control a force that drives a lot of people — *the need for acceptance*. But how do they do it? One woman summed it up like this: 'All I can do is be me. If someone doesn't like me, it's their choice. You can't be accepted by everyone. No matter how I change, there will always be someone else who won't accept me, so I may as well be me.' I thought back to the ironman scene. When I was around the 'cool' clique, I wasn't as close to the serious guys — and so it went on, around the circle.

I've found that people with silent power are genuinely happy with who they are and what they're becoming, and this sense of self-certainty is obvious and attractive to all who cross their path. It creates the presence I'd noticed. The certainty that comes with silent power provides a great base from which to take massive action, because you know that if something doesn't work out, it's to do with the action, not with you personally.

~ Is there a gap between who I am and how I want to be perceived?

~ Is it important for me to be accepted?

~ Are there any situations where I lose who I am by trying to be someone else?

PRINCIPLE SEVENTEEN

FIND YOUR 'WHY?'

'I'd like to talk to you about the seminar you gave here last Thursday.' The concern in his voice grabbed my attention.

'Sure, what do you want to talk about?'

'Well, on Friday morning four of my staff members resigned. Is that meant to happen?' I kept silent, knowing he hadn't finished. 'When I signed you, I didn't think it would cost me four staff members. I just wanted them to be more motivated.'

Now it was my turn. 'Would you mind if I ask *you* a few questions?'

'Sure,' he replied, without hesitation.

'Did you want me to motivate your staff, or to improve the performance of your business?'

'I guess I wanted you to improve my business by motivating my staff.'

'And do you have any motivated under-achievers on your team, the sort of people who are always pumped up and jumping around, but don't really achieve many results?'

'Yeah, we have a few. They're the nicest people on the team.'

'They usually are,' I agreed. 'But you'd agree, then, that motivation doesn't always lead to good results?'

'I guess so.' He was starting to understand what I was getting at.

'If all you want is a motivated team, just threaten to sack them all if they don't fire up and start doing better.' I was joking, but he took my point. I went on to explain what I'd done that Thursday in the seminar. 'My goal in your company is to improve your business, not to motivate your staff. A by-product of what I do is motivation. For the committed members of your team, the motivation will be directed back into their work. For the people who are just killing time in your company, hopefully the motivation will be directed outward, and with a bit of luck they'll leave, find something they really want to do, and stop wasting your time and energy.'

'So, you're talking about stripping away the dead wood?'

'Yeah, in a way. It's a win for you, but it's also a win for the people who leave,' I replied, not wanting to trivialise the people who'd gone.

'It's just a pain having to retrain another group of staff.'

'It'll all be worth it when you've built a team around you who actually want to be there. It'll bring you out of the time-wasting cycle that's been slowing your business down, using your energy to fix people who don't want to be fixed.'

'OK, thanks. I was just making sure this was meant to happen.'

'I don't aim to come in and encourage people to leave your company. But if they leave after spending two hours with me, then they were never there.'

'Motivation' is a word that's often misunderstood. I can't tell you the number of people I've met who say they are searching for motivation, as if it's the key that will unlock the door to their success. They look for techniques, for strategies and quick fixes, but they don't see that no matter how good the motivation, we can't motivate a cow to lay an egg, or a kangaroo to fly north for the winter.

I want to talk about motivation because it's the focus of so much attention in the achiever. 'I need to get motivated. How can I get some motivation? Why am I never fully motivated?' In its simplest terms, *motivation is wanting to do something with no self-imposed resistance*. When we lack motivation, we are in a state of mind where we are trying to get ourselves to do something another part of us doesn't want to do. Not being motivated is a state of conflict — part of us wants something and part of us doesn't, and we're torn between the two. We've already looked at the importance of minimising this internal conflict.

I prefer not to use the word 'motivation' in my work, because it implies that the solution for someone who's not achieving good results is to get them 'motivated', to give them a technique, but that approach ignores the bigger question. I only use the word 'motivation' as a signal. Unrestrained momentum, or 'motivation', is the natural state for a human being, and if we're missing it, it's a signal that something needs to change. This principle is exciting, because it contains the solution to creating unrestrained momentum: *you must create a big enough 'WHY?'*.

~

HAPPY ACHIEVERS ARE IN A STATE OF UNRESTRAINED MOMENTUM.

~

Think of the most driven achievers you know of. People like Thomas Edison, Marie Curie, Amelia Earhart, Mohammed Ali and Bill Gates all had an unshakeable vision, a vision that *couldn't* be eroded by doubters, or enemies, or even by the existing laws in some cases. How did they all remain so driven, so courageous and so passionate for so long? What was their secret?

I asked myself these questions over and over again, looking for complicated answers, when the answer was in front of me the whole time, so simple I hadn't been able to see it. They had all been consumed by *a reason big enough to keep them driving forward*. In each case, their 'WHY?' was so compelling that inaction created massive pain. Getting motivated wasn't a problem — in fact, they were likely to suffer from being over-motivated.

I'm not saying that these massive achievers never had an off day when they felt completely flat. When we pursue *anything* worthwhile, there are always days when taking action seems fruitless, when we doubt our strategies and the likelihood of achieving what we've set out to do. We're all human.

The difference between the massive achiever and the towel-thrower is that the massive achiever has a big enough 'WHY?' to help them punch through the days of frustration, doubt and lethargy.

The first reaction I have when someone tells me they're having trouble remaining 'motivated' is to ask, 'Why do you want it?' Invariably, the reason is nowhere near compelling enough to create massive action. Take exercise, for example. How often do you hear people say, 'I should exercise, but I can't get motivated in the mornings'? A very simple mind-set is at work here — namely, that there's more pain associated with getting up than with staying in bed. Many people pass this off as a lack of 'motivation', but I don't agree. They are motivated, *really* motivated — but it's to turn off the alarm, roll over and go back to sleep, and to think about exercising tomorrow.

Often, people fall victim to a belief system that says, 'I'm not the sort of person who can exercise.' The inference here is that they will *never* exercise consistently. Yet, the only thing they need if they *really* want to change is a compelling 'WHY?'.

A close friend of mine believed this for fifty years. He was a highly motivated guy — he approached drinking too much, eating junk food and never getting regular exercise with unrestrained momentum. He changed the day he discovered he needed triple heart bypass surgery. He's just as motivated now, but today he's got a big enough 'WHY?' to eat healthy food, to exercise and to look after himself.

Now, I'm not recommending this as the preferred strategy for finding *your* 'WHY?'. If he'd wanted to exercise and eat healthily, but had found himself unmotivated, the better strategy would have been to visit a few hospitals, speak to patients who were about to go into surgery, ask them about their habits and compare them to his own. He could easily have created his 'WHY?', rather than leave it to chance.

The same principle applies to our dreams and to the things we're determined to create. It's essential that we first create a reason so compelling, so absorbing and so consuming, that we literally feel like tearing the walls down to go after it.

A few months ago, I was going through what I'd call a slow patch in my own actions. I couldn't put my finger on what was causing it. I just knew that I wasn't as driven as usual. I sat down at my computer and typed one word — 'Why?'. The question wasn't, 'Why don't I feel as juiced up?' It was, 'Why am I doing this?' Then, 'What is it I'm trying to create and why?' And, 'What will it give me?'

I wrote and wrote, feeling each reason adding more and more fuel to the fire. As each reason and benefit appeared on the screen, I could feel my passion intensifying. Then I asked one final question: 'What will it give others? If I achieve what I'm setting out to achieve, how will it impact on others?'

This final question sent me over the edge. It struck me that the most driven people throughout history were those who felt that they were on a mission. For Gandhi, the pain of fasting for independence, or of personal persecution, paled in comparison to the result, should he succeed. His mission was much bigger than him, bigger than his own personal pain. He was fasting for every colonised Indian. The stories of many massive achievers speak loudly of the need to develop a 'WHY?' that's larger than just ourselves. Our passion is intensified when the people we love, even people we've never met, are the beneficiaries of what we do.

~

PROBLEMS BECOME INSIGNIFICANT IN THE CONTEXT OF CONTRIBUTION.

~

Developing a 'WHY?' that involves others is the key to extracting that extra twenty per cent when we really need it. And, more importantly, it gives our lives a mission and meaning. Unhappy achievers prove this principle time and time again. *If you're only doing it for yourself, forget about gaining fulfilment through achievement*. The pathway to Happily Achieving is to create a life that has meaning. Happily Achieving is having what you do affect others in a positive way.

The further into the exercise I went, the more intense I became and the more creative my reasons. I came up with ideas I'd never thought of before, and the longer I persisted, the more compelling the 'WHY?' became. By the time I'd exhausted my reasons, two hours had flown by and I felt focused like never before. I was re-primed for action.

I know it sounds a little 'out there', but don't write it off. Push yourself to try it before you pass judgment. Just let your mind go and really chase your reasons for doing what you do, or for doing what you want to do. It's easy to end up doing things without any real thought about why you're doing them. We all see people who are caught in the rut of doing things that no longer give them any juice in life, in their relationships, careers and health.

Remember the way the brain works: the conscious mind can only handle limited volumes of information, so, with so much going on, the brain commits to making large chunks of our operations subconscious. It does this by developing routines and habits.

What this means is that our brain takes aspects of our day-to-day behaviour and turns on the autopilot. We no longer have to think about them consciously to complete them successfully. Things like eating, walking and driving become second nature. We must be careful, therefore, not to allow the important parts of our lives to be ruled just by our subconscious mind. We must have the courage to question.

The decision I made while sitting at my computer was that if I could no longer find a compelling 'WHY?', I would find a career that would give me one. I sat down knowing that the next time I stood up, I'd either be a hundred times more passionate about what I'm doing now, or heading in a completely different direction.

~

LIFE ISN'T LONG ENOUGH TO LIVE WITHOUT BEING PASSIONATE ABOUT WHAT WE DO.

~

The 'WHY?' is the source of *any* 'motivation'. Finding and then always reminding ourselves of the 'WHY?' ensures that we keep the flame for what we do, or it pushes us to search out and embrace new passions.

Happily Achieving means striving for our vision, without resistance from within. In creating a compelling 'WHY?', we guarantee the passion, the persistence, the drive and the meaning. The 'WHY?' removes the resistance to unrestrained momentum.

When you're lacking in direction, or feeling unmotivated, ask yourself:

~ **What am I trying to create? And WHY?**

~ **How will it make me happy, while contributing to others' happiness?**

BELIEVE IN THE
X FACTOR

One minute, two minutes, three minutes... four... Surely he'd hit the wall. Even from where I was, in eighth place, I could see his lead increasing with every turn. He was so far in front. He'd made his move early, five minutes into the two-hour race, which is unusual. Most competitors wait to get a feel for their foes before making those race-winning choices.

I kept waiting for him to fall back into the field, but he was away. He didn't hit the wall, he didn't even slow down, he just kept on pulling away to the finish line. Even before the end of the race, my curiosity was peeking. How had he done it? I'd had no idea he was that good. I'd had no idea anyone in our sport had that sort of performance available to them. I'd raced against him for years and I'd never seen him destroy the rest of the field so convincingly. What had changed?

We always shared a room during races, so once all the media hype around the day's racing had died down we finally got a chance to sit down and catch up. 'What the hell was that?' I asked. 'That's not meant to happen. No one's meant to win *that* easily.'

He looked at me and smiled, the sort of smile that's just bursting with pride and contentment. Then, after a moment, as his mind worked to come up with an answer, a new expression began to creep across his face — wonderment. He wasn't going to be able to tell me what he'd done to create such an amazing performance, *because he didn't know.*

'It was incredible. I didn't feel any pain. It was the easiest race I've ever done. I've never felt anything like it in my whole life. It was like there were absolutely no limits on how hard I could push it. My body just responded and did whatever I asked of it. It was weird, mate!'

The more he thought about it, the more surprised and genuinely bewildered he became. He was on a massive high. After some more questions, he went on to explain that, during the race, time had no relevance, like it was either standing still or flying — he couldn't tell which. He couldn't remember much of the race and, as he cast his mind back, he said that for some reason, during the race, he'd thought a lot less than he usually did. In fact, it now seemed that it had been an almost entirely thoughtless experience. Then he said something I'd heard many times before. It seemed to mean nothing to him, but it grabbed me immediately. 'It was like I had access to something I've never had access to before. I don't know — I hope I can access it again at some stage.'

I've heard this type of thing explained in many different ways in my interviews. I've heard athletes talk of accessing an extra ten per cent, ironmen talk about the day the seas just opened up and allowed them easy passage, money market dealers talk about walking on to the floor and knowing what was going to happen ahead of time for hours at a stretch, and doctors and healers talk about going by their gut feelings straight to the source of their patients' ailments.

I remember hearing a story about Picasso. He explained that when he entered his studio, he would mentally take his past mentors and teachers in with him. Once he began planning his next work, he would ask them to 'leave'; and when he actually started putting brush to canvas, he would 'leave' the room himself.

The question all this poses is: What is it that we get access to when we have these amazing performances? What is it that we tap into when we have a gut feeling about danger that allows us to avoid it? What is it that has us call someone, unprompted, just when they really need us to? What is this thing called intuition? Where does this force, or intelligence, or whatever we choose to call it, come from? From inside us? Is it part of the brain's power? Or does it come from outside us? Is it *us*, or is it *everything around us*?

I've met some people who believe without a doubt that they know what IT is. One of them is a little old man who knocks on my door about every month or so on Saturday. I admire his passion for his religion, and sometimes we'll talk for up to an hour. He's convinced that the IT is Jehovah. In fact, he promises me that if I just read a few more of his magazines and finally attend one of the meetings he keeps inviting me to, that I too will know that IT is Jehovah.

I have another knowing friend who is a devout Catholic. He knows that IT is really God and that every now and then God decides to put His arm around your shoulder. He also knows that the little old man who knocks on my door every few weeks is wrong — in fact, he says that he's a fruitcake.

I also know people who practise the Eckankar faith. They call IT Sugmad. The human being who is closest to Sugmad is called the Living Eck Master, who also happens to be a guy named Harrold who lives in the United States. He travels the world sharing what he knows IT to be. Eckists know that people in other religions just can't see IT clearly. When I told my Jehovah's Witness friend about the Eckists, he asked me to pass on a few magazines and tell them about the next meeting. He couldn't believe they had it so wrong.

Some people I've met don't have a name for IT; they just know that it's all around us. Other people I've come across believe that if enough people meditate simultaneously and tap into IT, then world peace will follow. When I mentioned the Eckists to one of these believers, he rolled his eyes and said: 'I'll take you to one of *our* meetings — it'll blow you away.'

In speaking to all these people, one thing becomes really clear — no one can be absolutely sure what IT is. The only thing we can be sure of is that no explanation of IT is true for everyone. But too many people have experienced IT, in whatever form, for it not to be true. Whatever IT is, it's real, it's powerful and it defies explanation.

~

THERE IS A HIGHER POWER AT THE CORE OF LIFE.

~

This is crucial to Happily Achieving, for a couple of reasons. First, no matter how diverse these belief systems are, they all have one thing in common, *faith* — that unique blend of thought and emotion inspired by the feeling that *there is something greater at work*.

Throughout history, faith has kept us moving forward and evolving. Word has been spread, tides have been turned, and great cities have been built on faith. Faith has been the most enduring and powerful of all human emotions. We're willing to act, to take massive action, *out of faith*.

In tapping into the feeling that everything will work out, that whatever is happening is part of the bigger picture, disappointment disappears, fear disappears, anxiety and frustration disappear, and we can power through all the things that inhibit the happy flow towards our goals.

~

WITH FAITH, WE FIND THE COURAGE TO MOVE HAPPILY TOWARDS OUR GOALS.

~

So often, all we need is one action backed by the faith that it will work out and the belief that, if it doesn't, it's because there is a greater plan at work. With that faith, there are no negatives. Happy Achievers believe that they are not alone. Their faith in a higher power makes them feel connected and gives their experiences, both good and bad, meaning.

Second, I've come to believe in what I call the *X factor*. It's the thing my ironman friend tapped into the day he won by such an incredible margin; the thing that allows the money market dealer to have that sense of 'knowing' when he walks on to the trading floor. The *X factor* is the force that we tap into when we do or know things that defy explanation. It's what creates amazing performances.

I have seen enough amazing performances and spoken to enough outstanding performers to be certain that the *X factor* exists and that it is part of those extreme achievements — but I have no proof. The only tangible indicator that I can point to is that feeling we've all had at times, in one way or another — such as when we find the solution to that unsolvable problem, or we experience inspired wisdom when advising someone in need, or when we experience unbelievable coincidences. Of course, all of this can be explained away as a fluke or chance. It's a matter of whether you choose to believe — whether you have faith.

~

MASSIVE ACHIEVERS ARE ABLE TO ACCESS SOMETHING BIGGER THAN THEMSELVES.

~

So, how do massive achievers access this mysterious force? Again, I can't tell you. What I *can* tell you is when it *won't happen*. It doesn't seem to happen when we don't believe. I've yet to see or hear of an extreme performance by someone who didn't believe that it was possible that an outstanding performance was inside them, waiting to break out.

In our hearts we all have a code that we live by, our own set of rules by which we play the game. It's very difficult to access extreme performance if we are breaking our own code by, say, treating people poorly when we believe that people should be treated with respect, cheating when we believe in fair play, reacting in fear when we believe in acting with courage. The *X factor* is available to us *only when we are being who we are in our soul — when we are true to ourselves and our beliefs*.

Happily Achieving and the *X factor* are one and the same. In my experience, it's impossible to Happily Achieve without being true to who we are and to what is important to us. We decide what we believe and what we don't believe. However 'alternative', 'strange', 'enlightened' or 'mainstream' they may be, Happy Achievers believe in some purpose that is greater than themselves.

Many people believe in a higher purpose; however, Happy Achievers are confident enough in their own beliefs that they don't feel the need to convert others to their way of thinking. They understand that what they believe may only be right for them, and that trying to win someone over to their beliefs doesn't make them any more right or true. Happy Achievers know that, as far as faith is concerned, there is no right or wrong, there are only differences.

Wouldn't it be sad to think that this is it? We come, we go; we exist without meaning, without some place in a bigger picture. Who knows? I certainly don't. All I can tell you is that it doesn't make me any happier, or any more effective, to believe that we've seen all there is to see, that this really is IT. To me, that's what it comes down to:

Happy Achievers believe in something greater than themselves because, right or wrong, true or false, this faith makes them happy and enables them to achieve at — and sometimes above — their best.

~ **What do *you* believe?**

PRINCIPLE NINETEEN

LIVE IN THE NOW

I'd been working really hard, so when the opportunity came up unexpectedly to take a skiing trip, I jumped at the chance. I love skiing, and the thought of the cold, fresh air on my face as I jetted down the slopes was definitely exciting. All week I looked forward to my holiday. I thought about the mountains, the resort, the partying, and the friends I'd be sharing it with. Every possible scenario for fun raced through my mind.

The week dragged, but the day finally arrived. The snow was fantastic, even better than I'd hoped for, and the conditions were perfect. During the day, I'd look forward to dinner that night; and at dinner, with all my friends around having a great time, I'd be thinking about the skiing the next day. Come the following day, I'd be out on the snow focusing again on dinner that night. The same thing happened day after day. I was so keyed up not to miss anything, that I found myself in a constant cycle of looking forward.

When I got home, I realised something that scared me. I began to think about the trip and it was like every memory had been condensed into one moment. I felt completely dissociated. It was as if someone else had taken the trip. I had the memories, but no feelings about those memories. Slowly, what had happened started to dawn on me: I'd been focusing on the future for the whole trip, and as a consequence I'd missed the present, the NOW. I'd been so excited about what was *going to happen*, that I'd missed what was *actually going on at the time*. I'd missed my own holiday.

Then I had a really uncomfortable thought, the kind that has the potential to change your life: 'My whole life is like that. I'm constantly focused on the future. I'm always looking forward to what's *about to happen*, and I'm always thinking about what I'm *trying to achieve*.'

A truly horrible thought followed, the kind that *definitely* changes your life. I pictured some of the nursing homes I'd visited and saw myself at age eighty, lying in one of the beds. I was thinking about my life, and the entire eighty years were condensed into a single moment in time. I had no feelings about it whatsoever. It was like watching a movie with the sound turned down. Images of my life drifted past, but they didn't seem to have any connection to me. I was hollow. It was scary stuff.

I had to think. I sat quietly for a few hours and, after a while, I realised that as much as I wanted to achieve in my life, as much as I wanted to improve my situation, and despite all the positive reasons I wanted to move forward and have more choices, *I was missing my life.*

The more I thought about it, the more obvious it became that my life up until now had been lived as a kind of preparation for later, for the life I'd live once I'd reached my goals. This pattern had to go. If I was lucky, I'd have ninety years, and that's hardly long enough to get the most out of life as it is. I knew what I had to do.

The conscious mind has three choices when it comes to what you focus on — the past, the present, or the future — and the challenge we face as achievers is to spend as much time as possible in the present. The temptation is to live for the future, like I did, or to dwell in the past. How many times have you missed a gorgeous view, or the smell of a barbecue, or a really good conversation because you were re-running yesterday's meeting in your head? How many times do you miss the connection with the one you love most in the world because you're caught in the past or the future?

It's common to hear the elderly talk of having their priorities confused when they were younger, of coming home to the people they loved most in the world after a tough day, only to leave their minds at the office all night — a surefire recipe for frustration. 'But you don't understand,' they would say, 'I'm doing it for you.' 'I just want you and your mind together in the same place,' their partner would reply. They missed the juiciest part of their life, and the really sad thing is that, by the time many of them realise it, it's too late to do anything about it.

~

WE MUST SPEND OUR TIME IN THE NOW.

~

Being sensitive to the simple things that make our level of fulfilment in life greater is one of the skills we must develop if we're going to Happily Achieve. How often do we take the little things for granted? Sights like steam snaking off a hot, wet road; waves breaking on the beach; the colours in a cloud at sunset; or the sound of someone we love laughing; the wind in the trees; our partner's soft breathing next to us; or rain hitting the roof when we're warm in bed; the taste of a meat pie on a winter's day or an ice cream on a scorcher; or the smell of mum's roast in the oven. All of these things make our lives richer, and we miss so many of them.

Our lives are happening NOW. It's too easy to miss the important stuff. If we can gain pleasure from these basic things, we don't have to have a fortune to love life, and we won't *need* achievement in order to be happy.

We must be emotionally independent of our goals. We must set ourselves up to be happy, regardless of our achievements. The pressure and the stress that comes with investing all our happiness in a particular outcome kills the joy in life, because shit happens and things don't always go the way we plan.

~

HAPPY ACHIEVERS DON'T HAVE THEIR HAPPINESS RIDING ON THE RESULT, BECAUSE THEY'RE NOT ACHIEVING TO BE HAPPY.

~

Unfortunately, too many people believe that 'the hungry wolf hunts harder', so they deprive themselves of the truly juicy emotions until they achieve. But, as we have seen throughout this book, this is a perfect set-up for getting knocked over by a massive let-down.

The best way to Happily Achieve is to use juicy emotions, rather than 'at all costs' emotional stakes like fear, anxiety and stress. Achieving either way is possible, but spending the majority of your time living in the NOW means that you give yourself the greatest chance of spending your journey experiencing the juiciest emotions, because living in the NOW has the most incredible, immediate impact on the feelings we experience today. The better you feel, the greater will be your capacity to achieve.

Imagine how you would feel every day if you noticed that first eye contact with your partner in the morning. Imagine if you started noticing when someone smiled at you or gave you a compliment.

Imagine actually slowing down long enough to enjoy the smell of your neighbour's flowers as you pass in the morning, or taking the time to listen to more music, or stretch out in the sun. Imagine seeing those friends you wish you had more time for, more often.

~ Imagine being blind, and suddenly seeing.

ATTACK YOUR LIFE'S DREAM

I wondered whether I'd made a mistake. I looked at Monique and I could tell she was having the same doubts. 'We *have* to do this, right?' She didn't answer. Instead, she took my hand and we stepped out of the elevator. The hallway was white and gleaming, shiny clean. Too clean. As we moved away from the elevator we smelled that unmistakable smell, faint at first, then overpowering — industrial-strength antiseptic. It was everywhere, masking everything but the real smell, the reason we were here.

I could feel my stomach turning. There was nowhere to hide under the harsh fluorescent lights. We were two floors underground and I could feel the weight of the concrete above us, as though my shoulders were supporting the whole building.

Fear and adrenaline pumped through me as the smell grew stronger the closer we got. We both stopped before knocking on the door, as if it was our last chance to reconsider our commitment to do what we'd come to do. Monique had wanted to come. She'd joked about the places I'd asked her to visit on our dates. She's so full of courage. I was glad to have her company because I knew she'd see things differently. We'd be learning together; it would double the experience.

We had come to see death. A few days before, I'd been flicking through a book and one page caught my attention. I'm not sure of the exact wording, but the message was simple: to understand life, we must first understand death. I wanted to understand more than anything else, but I had no idea where to start. The answer was simple. I had to see death.

I'd called the morgue, expecting to have to do some serious explaining, but the attendant hadn't hesitated to make an appointment for the next day. I guess live visitors were a nice change.

I remember noticing a distinct lack of sound in that hallway. Absolute silence, except for the hum of the air-conditioners. When I finally knocked on the door, the sound thundered down the hall and echoed back. Our chance to pull out had passed, and our breathing seemed very loud in the ensuing quiet.

It took him an age to answer the door, plenty of time for my imagination to run wild. I expected to be greeted by a tall, skinny, pale man in a dark suit, with a tape measure around this neck. The door opened with a jolt.

'Hi. Andrew, is it?' The attendant was young and fresh-faced. He couldn't have been further from what I'd imagined. 'Come on in.'

He welcomed us into his office, eager to talk, and we sat down. I wanted to get an idea of the belief systems that would allow him to work around death every day. Most people will do anything in their power to avoid even the thought of it. Death is something that happens to other people. It's a news bulletin from far-away places that has nothing to do with their families and friends. This young man was constantly reminded of the reality of death, since it rolled through his door with painful regularity.

'How do you cope with being around death so much?' I asked.

'Upstairs we have the live-stock,' he said, referring to the maternity ward. 'They start the journey up there and finish it down here. If we don't have the dead-stock, we don't have the live-stock. That's how I see it, anyway.'

'If you believed something else, would it be hard for you to work down here? Does it ever get to you?' It was quiet while he searched for an answer.

'I don't like it when the little kids come in. That gets to me. They don't deserve to visit here.' The quiet returned and I wondered whether he could be happy staying in this job forever.

'You want to have a look around?' We followed him out of the office and in the direction of a steel door. The door opened without a sound, revealing a stainless steel room. The floor, the walls, the ceiling and the tools were all smooth, sleek steel.

'This is the room where we do the autopsies.' He picked up various tools and explained what they were used for. 'This is the tool we use to extract the brain from the skull,' he said, handling a strange circular blade. My stomach turned again. He spoke clinically about his work, and I guessed that he was in the emotional state he had conditioned himself to be in in order to do his job in this room. Any emotional reaction would make his job too difficult.

He must have known the reactions we were having, but I'd asked to see death, so his attitude seemed to be, 'If they want to see death, I'll show them death.' He didn't spare us.

Eventually, he sensed that we'd had enough, so we moved to the other side of the room and to another door. Again, it swung open in perfectly oiled silence. The smell, the one the antiseptic couldn't quite hide, poured over us in a wave. We'd arrived at the source.

'This is where we keep them after the autopsy.' The refrigeration room — rows and rows of shiny metal doors, five along and three deep. 'They're taken from here to their final resting place.' The still, stale, cold smell of death clung to the room and everything in it.

The attendant was ready to keep moving, but I stopped. 'Can we see one of the bodies?' Even as I asked the question, my stomach flipped and I had to fight off nausea. I was determined to follow through. I needed to learn what I'd come here to learn.

'If you want.' The attendant smiled, a little surprised. 'We only have one here at the moment. I just finished working on him before you arrived. He committed suicide this morning.'

He opened a fridge and rolled out the body of a man in his early forties. I felt numb. At that moment, I could have felt any one of a thousand different emotions . . . and I felt numb. Until it hit me. Anger flooded in and overcame the numbness. How could he have wasted something so valuable as his life? How could he have given up on something so priceless? What right did he have?

Then, just as quickly, my rage gave way to overwhelming sympathy. Why couldn't someone just have reached out to this man? How could it have gotten so bad? And my sympathy turned to a sense of helplessness. I pride myself on trying to help where I can, and for the first time in my life I was seeing someone I couldn't do anything for. There was no going back — his decision was final. It was crushing . . .

All of these thoughts and emotions flashed through me in a matter of moments, and I was then calm again. I reached out and touched his arm. It was cold and dry. My touch left a small indent that would never bounce back. I looked deeply into his face and I was struck. Whatever it was that we call 'life' had gone. 'Life' didn't seem to weigh anything.

He was the same weight on the shelf as he had been when he was alive that morning. But something was missing. Where had it gone? So many questions without answers, questions I'd never asked before.

For the first time in my life I was confronted by the fragility of the line between life and death. It's so easily moved. Four hours earlier, the body in front of me had been alive, a walking, talking, breathing, functioning human being, warm with life. Not ten years ago, but at nine o'clock that morning, as I'd been eating my morning bowl of cornflakes. Now his life was over. It was really hard to process.

Regardless of your beliefs about the after-life, this man's body was a testament to the finality of his last decision. It was this finality that I was having the most difficulty grappling with. He couldn't talk his way out of this one. He couldn't say he was sorry and start again. He would never again have the luxury of regret. He was finished.

I was suddenly being shown my life from a different angle, as if looking back. I'd spent so much time preparing the foundations of my future enjoyment, worrying about the success of this or the possible failure of that, waking in the night sweating with concern for some project that wasn't proceeding the way I wanted it to. I was wasting away as a result of focusing on petty problems. I wasn't who I should have been ... I wasn't who I wanted to be.

Perspective ... Death taught me perspective. It gave me the opportunity to see life, *my* life, through clear eyes. We spend so much time on unnecessary tasks, and place so much importance on irrelevant things, that it costs us the joy of the moment. Death was teaching me to live.

I started thinking about the people who live defensively their entire lives, afraid of what life might throw at them. It's so easy to let the fear motivate us that we start protecting what we have, rather than going after what we really want. We don't feel the moment when the balance shifts, when avoiding pain becomes more important than moving towards pleasure. We fall into the habit of preparing for something to go wrong, spending too much of our lives worrying about when it will happen. We get too busy to see that we're in a constant state of 'prepared defence'. And finally we choke on the fear, the fruit of the defensive mentality.

In the presence of death, my 'defences' made me sick to the stomach. I was humbled. Slowly, I understood the truth that death made clear: *life is about being on the attack.* It's about doing what you really want to be doing, taking that trip, starting that project, putting yourself on the line, all the while knowing that you may only be four hours away from lying on a slab in a steel fridge. Attacking life is keeping your life's vision clear and colourful, even when it seems easier to let it go. It's about moving towards the pleasure, regardless of the pain.

Life is an amusement park with so many rides we could never fit them all into one day, but we have to try. Attacking life is about doing things just because you've never done them before; it's about searching for new and different experiences every day to ensure that the relentless pressures of routine don't take the reins of your life and drive away the juice.

Attacking life means that you have the courage to take a broom to the things that aren't important and sweep them away, staying true to the essentials of your life, no matter what the cost. It's about refusing to delay the process of becoming who you want to be, and about not allowing yourself to become one of the 'living dead' — a person with all the signs of human existence, but no signs of life. I had no idea when I was flipping through my book that what I would read there would ring so true. Death *does* teach us to live.

Death teaches us about the value of our achievements. What we achieve means nothing in the face of death. The truly vital thing is what achievement makes us — who we become. Achievement is just a tool, a tool for growth and personal development. Achievement is a tool for living. It's a reason to explore a wider range of emotions and experiences in the limited time we have.

I learned the real importance of Happily Achieving in that morgue. I walked away convinced that there are no guarantees in life — and that means that we owe it to ourselves to enjoy what is happening in our lives NOW.

Sometimes I sit and dream. I dream about a world where each one of us is able to live a life not of fear, but of courage. A world where we can all go after the things we love and the life we want, filled with an unquenchable yearning to live our lives to the maximum.

I thank you for reading this book and for investing this time in yourself. I ask that you not let this book be just another tool that lies gathering dust on the shelf. Let this book give you power. Let it give you knowledge. But most importantly, let it help you to take action. Let it be the spark that fires you into doing what you know you would love to do.

~

GO AFTER WHATEVER IT IS THAT JUICES YOU, AND HAVE AN ABSOLUTE BALL DOING IT. MY HEART IS WITH YOU.

~